"Splendid and sordid, sneaky and forthright, jaded and full of hope. Malone has tremendous powers of observation, and these detailed, plain-mouthed tales have big, beating hearts."

—ROBIN ROMM, author of *The Mercy Papers* and *The Mother Garden*

. . .

"A stunning debut. Somehow Malone manages to be both gutsy and subtle at once — her characters are complicated, messed up in the very best way, and full of depth. Malone's prose is a gorgeous combination of lyricism and colloquialism — a tightrope she walks with skill. *People Like You* is full of people like us with all of our sorrows, fears, our wit and damage, and this debut collection deserves many, many readers and high praise!"

—LISA GLATT, author of *The Nakeds* and *A Girl Becomes a Comma Like That*

. . .

"Margaret Malone's masterfully constructed stories simmer with a dry, dark humor that reveals the truth of the human soul. *People Like You* makes good on the promise of its title, with characters who are fully formed heads and hearts and bodies struggling with loneliness, love (or lack thereof), and who — and how — to *be* in the modern world."

—LIZ PRATO, author of *Baby's on Fire*

Margaret Malone

PEOPLE LIKE YOU

Margaret Malone's writing has appeared in *The Missouri Review, Propeller Quarterly, Coal City Review, Swink, Nailed,* latimes.com, and elsewhere, including the Forest Avenue Press anthology *The Night, and the Rain, and the River.* She is the recipient of fellowships from the Oregon Arts Commission and Literary Arts, two Regional Arts & Culture Council Project Grants, and residencies at The Sitka Center and Soapstone. Malone has a degree in philosophy from Humboldt State University. She lives with her husband filmmaker Brian Padian and two children in Portland, where she co-hosts the artist and literary gathering SHARE.

MargaretMalone.com

PEOPLE LIKE YOU

stories

Margaret Malone

ATELIER26 BOOKS
Portland, Oregon

Cover design by Nathan Shields
Interior design by M.A.C.

isbn-13: 978-0-9893023-6-4
isbn-10: 0989302369

Library of Congress Control Number: 2015943384

The following stories have been previously published,
in slightly different form: "People Like You" (*Coal City
Review*), "The Only One" (*Propeller Quarterly*), "Yes"
(*The Timberline Review*), "The Things We Know
Nothing About" (*Nailed*), "Saving the Animals" *(The
Night, and the Rain, and the River,* Forest Avenue Press,
2014, ed. Liz Prato), "Sure Footing" (*Rhapsoidia*).

Atelier26 Books are printed in the U.S.A. on
acid-free paper.

Atelier26

*"A magnificent enthusiasm, which feels
as if it never could do enough to reach
the fullness of its ideal; an unselfishness
of sacrifice, which would rather cast
fruitless labour before the altar than
stand idle in the market."*—John Ruskin

Atelier26Books.com

For my dad,
John S. Malone,
who loves books in general
and short stories in particular

CONTENTS

PEOPLE LIKE YOU

PEOPLE LIKE YOU

The invitation is from a friend, though I use this term loosely: we have no friends. We have acquaintances from work, or old friends who live in other cities, or people who used to be our friends who we either borrowed money from and never repaid or who we just never bother to call anymore because we decided we either don't like them or we're too good for their company. We are not perfect.

Along with the invite is a small slip of paper with typed directions to the party at their house and one phone number, the cell, to *RSVP to,* and one phone number, the land line, to *absolutely not RSVP to.*

The rest of the mail, all advertisements and credit card offers in white envelopes with plastic windows, I dump onto the kitchen table next to my gin and tonic.

"Another party," I say. "How will we ever find the time?"

Bert says, "Be nice."

Bert is lurking at the other corner of the kitchen table in running shorts and tube socks, finally reading this morning's newspaper, drinking root beer from a can. He sticks a Post-it on an article he wants to remember to come back to later and read.

He says, "Whose?"

I will never understand why he doesn't just read the newspaper article he wants to read when he wants to read it. If we ever actually divorce, this will be a big reason why.

"It's a surprise party," I say. "For Gerry, from Nan."

I sip my gin and tonic. The ice cubes jingling against the glass.

Then I say, "We have to go. We never go anywhere. We are going."

It is up to me to RSVP to the party, and I don't like talking to people on the phone: no facial gestures or body language, just one voice, then another voice, then the first voice again. So I wait to call and RSVP as long as I can.

I wait until the morning of the party.

When I call the number to RSVP to, Nan's cell, Nan is curt, using monosyllabic responses that have nothing to do with what I am saying.

"Sorry to RSVP so late," I say.

"Yes," she says. "Okay."

"But we're definitely coming tonight."

"Uh huh," she says. "Yes. No, I can hear you."

I say, "It's Cheryl and Bert." It's been a long time since we've seen them. I say again, "Bert and Cheryl. It's Cheryl."

"Great," she says. "Yes, I hear you just fine now."

"Okay then," I say. "So, bye."

Bert and I decide we need to leave early because we are always late and it's a surprise party and we don't want to ruin it like we joke that we might.

We are getting dressed. Bert is in his beige dress socks and worn plaid boxers, and I am putting on my black stockings and watching my boobs in the mirror. My boobs are just hanging there, swinging around a bit, waiting to have their bra put on. And Bert says, "Watch. Something will happen and we'll end up getting there at the same time as Gerry. And he'll be like, 'Hey guys? What are you doing here? This is so weird.' Then Gerry's voice will drop an octave," Bert says, "and he'll be like, 'Oh my god.' And we'll be like 'No, no. We're here looking at a ... house to buy in the area.'"

I'm putting a leg into my skirt and I say, "Yeah, then Gerry will be like 'A house. Around here? Oh, with the money that you never paid back?'"

Bert puts on his pants. He says, "Right. And then he'll be like, 'It's a surprise party isn't it. It's a goddamned surprise party and now I know.' Then he'll be like, 'Thanks a lot, you jackholes.' Gerry always says that. 'You jackholes,' he'll say."

And I'm brushing my teeth and Bert's in his slippers running mousse through his hair and we both start laughing. These are the best times. I love these times.

We're in the car. We're on the freeway. For once there's no tension. I am me, driving, and he is him, sitting there.

"Which exit?" I say.

Bert checks the small white slip included in our invitation and says, "Canoga Park Boulevard. Where the hell is that?"

I cordially suggest he consult the Thomas Guide but Bert refuses.

"It's coming up here," he says. "No, wait. That's Canoga Ave."

"Right," I say.

"That's definitely a different exit," says Bert.

"Yes," I say. "Altogether."

We drive in silence for minutes, the inside-car hush of our motion, all the best-times feelings dissolving, the thick familiar air starts up between us. Me, driving. Him, sitting there.

"Watch," says Bert. "That was probably the exit. There's probably the wrong directions printed on all the invites."

"That'd be funny," I say.

We drive to Thousand Oaks before Bert looks in the Thomas Guide, finds the street index in the back of the spiral-bound atlas, and sees there is no Canoga Park Blvd. exit anywhere in southern California.

We turn around.

"Of course," says Bert. "Of fucking course."

We know we're now going back the right way, but night is creeping up, and I am wearing a skirt, and we're in a car on the freeway in the middle of the god-forsaken San Fernando Valley. On the little slip that says *Exit Canoga Park Blvd.* it also says *Call if you get lost.* This is the same number, the land line, to *absolutely not RSVP to.* I call. I want Nan to know that she screwed up the directions and hopefully feel bad and say nice things to us even though she's in the middle of hosting a surprise party.

Phone ringing.

"Nan?" I say. "It's Cheryl. We're lost. There is no Canoga Park Boulevard exit."

"Canoga Park?" she says. "You mean Canoga Ave.? Sure there is."

I'm wanting to be nice, but I am driving seventy miles per hour and talking on the phone, and this is why we don't leave the house. So what I'm also wanting is to say what's the point of printing up directions to a place and including them in an invitation if the directions are wrong? You think someone would check a thing like that.

"We're on our way," I say.

"Watch," says Bert. "We'll get there and I bet nobody

else had any trouble finding the place. They'll be like, 'No, not a lick of trouble. Found it fine.' Bastards."

Bert does not like to be lost. It's the man in him.

We drive. Back the way we came. Headlights and tail-lights and setting sun all battle for my attention. We pass the same landmarks, the long perfect row of leafy eucalyptus trees, the lit-up cross on top of an empty hill, the dull box of a building with the banner saying *If you worked here, you'd be at work by now.*

Something is wrong.

"I checked every goddamn sign," I say. "There was no Canoga Ave."

"Me too," says Bert. The overhead light comes on and he consults the Thomas Guide, finds the page with the map of where we are. "There is no Canoga Ave. exit in this direction. It's only going the other way."

I'm trying to stay calm.

We exit somewhere. We call again.

"Nan? Cheryl. No Canoga Ave. exit this way. We're lost. I have no idea where we are." I'm using the tone that Bert calls testy. "Is Gerry there yet? Did we miss it?" And I don't even care. I hope he's come so we can say we tried, we missed it, and turn around and go home.

"No, you've still got twenty minutes," she says. "No, ten minutes now. Maybe you should wait. No. Just come. Look for balloons. If there are balloons out front, he's still not here."

"Not sure where we are," I say.

I'm not trying hard enough not to be rude.

"Don't know how long we'll be," I say. My phone snaps shut.

We drive.

"Nan says to look for balloons," I tell Bert. "If there are balloons then Gerry's not there yet."

"Wait," Bert says. "What? Don't you think Gerry coming home and seeing balloons is a dead giveaway? Don't you think he'll pick up on that?"

I contemplate how this might work. "No. Wait," I say. "It makes sense. They take the balloons in before he gets back."

"Who does?" says Bert.

"I don't know. Nan does. Nan takes the balloons in."

"How does she know?" says Bert.

"I don't know. Nan is psychic. How do I know? Maybe they have a lookout or something. Fucking fuck!"

Under an overpass, there is a stop sign. We can go left, go right, go straight. It is dark. We are somewhere in the Valley.

I say, "Straight?"

Bert says, "Left. No, right."

I go straight.

Two streets up, on the corner, is a giant neon bowling pin and underneath is a neon arrow pointing to a building that says Canoga Avenue Bowl. We go left. We go right, then right. There are balloons.

We try to get out of our croaky-doored Honda, but a car drives up behind us.

"Get down," Bert says. "It could be Gerry."

The car drives past. We try again. More cars keep coming.

Each time we see headlights we duck down in our seats so an oncoming car won't see our heads. We're determined to not ruin the surprise. Or maybe allow ourselves the opportunity to go home without being seen.

Twenty-seven pairs of headlights later Bert's had enough. He yells, "Screw it."

We get out of the car.

. . .

We walk into the party. We don't know anybody. It's a very small house.

Nan sees us. She waves a big wave in our direction from the snack table. Her voice singsongs over the noise of the people we don't know talking. She's still waving. She says, "Gerry's on his way."

I look around the party and realize two things. One, I hate parties. Parties are strangers and someone else's idea of music and the overt pressure to talk to the strangers over the volume of the music while appearing to have a good time. Two, there are three other women present, and they are all pregnant. A tender spot: my eggs are no good.

We head for the booze.

This is when Gerry walks in and we all yell, *Surprise!* He looks awful. Gerry used to be really chubby and sweet, always smiling, the best man to hug. But he's been dieting and exercising, getting into shape. Seeing the unfamiliar angles of his revealed chin, his jaw and cheekbones makes him unrecognizable. I can't help but think he looks gaunt, almost unhealthy. When I go to say hello and happy birthday what I want to say is, "I liked you better before." It takes all my willpower not to tell him this. When he smiles, I want to feed him.

Also, he doesn't look surprised. Nan notices.

She says, "Did you know? You didn't know."

And Gerry says, "Well, there are balloons out front. Also, Bill told me on the way." Gerry points to his brother Bill, who is a younger and shorter still-pudgy Gerry, with long hair pulled back in a ponytail, and who is so drunk his feet shuffle like he's on the deck of ship caught in a storm. "I didn't even ask," Gerry says. "We were at a stoplight coming back from sushi and Bill turns down the radio and yells 'Surprise! It's a surprise.'"

Nan is calm. Then Nan punches Bill in the neck. He

falls over, smiling, too shit-faced to have any idea how many things he's just done wrong. Nan gets him some ice.

She says, "It's a party," to remind me and Bert and the other people why we're here.

I pretend I'm standing here drinking a beer, but really I am surveying the landscape. A clump of people on the couch, more in the hallway, and a cluster of the rest of everyone standing at the snack table. Bert and me, we are in the cluster. There is music coming from the bedroom in the back of the small house, and a potato-looking guy in a faded Rush tee-shirt is next to me, talking and talking, the kind of person that talks about whatever is on his mind, no matter who he is talking to. He's telling me and Bert and whoever squeezes past us for a pig-in-a-blanket about his car, a Grand Am, and what it can do.

"If I had to, in an emergency, I could roll it, and the car would be fine." He raises his eyebrows to emphasize how serious he is. "Seriously," he says. "Fine."

I make my eyes really big, like *wow, Grand Ams, awesome*, and then he starts to laugh and I don't know if he's laughing at himself or at me, but he laughs so hard his laugh turns into a cough. While he is coughing, I excuse myself without saying so. Bert is right behind me.

We head away from the snack table, somewhere safe. Wending our way through the living room, Bert says, "At least now I know I'm not the biggest asshole here."

There is no line for the bathroom, so we walk right in, lock the door. Bert closes the lid of the toilet and takes a seat on the shag cover, his feet on the matching rug. I lean against the cabinet of the sink. It's always a good idea to have a destination at a party, some specific location in place of the headless wandering from one point to another trying to find the something you have in common with someone else.

The last person in here splashed water all over the counter. "People are pigs," I say. I mop up the mess with a terry cloth hand towel.

I say, "I think I left my drink somewhere."

I say, "Should we have sex?"

Bert throws some beer down his throat. He says, "I'm missing Law & Order right now. I don't know. Do you want to?"

"Sure," I say. "In a second." Bert selects a magazine from the reading material in a basket on the tile floor.

Above the sink is a mirror that is really a medicine cabinet. I look inside. There are Q-tips and orange pill bottles and toothpaste and a razor dirty with stubble bits and tweezers. The top shelf is all make-up. I close my eyes and rub silvery shadow in the soft crease above my lashes.

Bert does not look up from the magazine. He says, "It says that horses sleep standing up. That's not right. I've seen them lying down. This is wrong."

There are Band-Aids and nail polish remover and dental floss, and even though I don't know what else I'm looking for, nothing looks good. I unspool some floss. "Want some?" Bert says no. He reads and I floss between my teeth. There is a knock at the door.

Straight for the bar, that's where I head. Bert, of course, right behind me. The bar is really the kitchen counter, which is where the bottles and red plastic cups are set up. I am running my tongue over my teeth, which feel so clean now. Next to me and Bert is one of the pregnant women, pouring herself a club soda.

"The bubbles," she says. "You know." She points to her stomach.

Somewhere I heard pregnancy makes women kind of stupid, the body so busy doing other stuff it doesn't have time to send smarts to the brain. So, I'm not missing out on that. But Bert and me, our life is at a standstill. A baby would really be something. To the pregnant woman, I want to say, *If I wash my hands can I touch your big belly?*

"Watch," Bert says. He is reaching over me to grab the plastic bottle of vodka. "We're going to be stuck here for, like, two hours."

I want to say, *Because maybe some of your babyness will rub off on me.*

Bert is muttering. He says, "The house is so small, we'll never be able to leave."

I want to say, *Or maybe when your baby is born, I could come over and hold her in my arms, and your baby could tell my unborn baby that it's okay to come down now, it's okay?*

Bert sticks his face into his red plastic cup and sips. He says, "I should be in my pajamas right now." He heads back for the snack table.

Standing next to the front door, by a long, narrow table with presents on it, is Nan, and this reminds me that we didn't bring a present for Gerry. I grab a beer from the fridge and head right for her.

I hug her when I get there, because that's what people do. Maybe Nan will apologize about the directions. If she doesn't mention it, I'm not going to either. I'm going to be big about it.

I say, "We left Gerry's present at home."

"That's okay," Nan says. But I can tell she doesn't believe me.

I gulp down half my beer. We look out at the party.

"Great party," I say.

The glass bottle feels really heavy. Bert is still at the snack table. Alone in the crowd, his hand in the pretzel bowl.

"Too bad about those directions," I say. The beer slides smooth down my throat. I polish off the bottle.

Nan doesn't say anything back. She must not have heard me. I can see that she is watching Gerry in the clump of people on the couch. He's laughing, his eyes crinkled up like closed fists.

I shake my empty at Bert across the room. He raises his bottle like we're toasting from far away. I try again. I turn my empty bottle upside down, make a sad face. He stuffs a handful of pretzels into his mouth, wipes his hands on his pants, and aims his body for the fridge.

Finally, Nan turns her attention to me. She says, "Thanks for coming, Cheryl."

"You know," I say. "Because they were all wrong, we couldn't figure them out."

Bert heads our way with a full beer. Thank God. I hope he's driving back.

There is a knock at the front door and Nan turns to answer it. I haven't asked her about Gerry yet, about where all that fat went. Have to remember to ask her before we leave. The beer is full and cold and the sip I take is too big, and as it's going down, I can tell that I just crossed the rushing river of my drink quota, and there will be no going back.

Nan says to the open door, "Finally! No, I'm kidding. Coats on the bed in back."

More people we don't know. I smile at them, at least there's another woman here.

I say, "You pregnant too?"

Bert squeezes my arm before the blond can answer. He pulls me toward the snack table and I think I forgot to eat because I can feel the beer sloshing around inside me when I move.

The beer bottle in my hand is too much, it's weighing me down, so I take a last, big drink, goodbye beer, and look around for a spot nearby, somewhere flat, to drop it off.

That's when I notice them in the hallway between the bathroom and the bedroom. Their round heads bumping the ceiling. They are blue and red and yellow and green. Long ribbons tied together, hanging down. I have the urge to stick them with a pin. I have the urge to set them free, watch them sail away into the dark sky until I cannot see them anymore.

Behind me, Bert says, "Where are you going?"

It's easy to ignore him.

When I pass the balloons in the hall, I wrap my hand around the ribbons and pull them through the open doorway with me into the bedroom where Bill, Gerry's brother, is passed out on the bed, red welt on his neck, curled up with the pile of coats. Even though Bill has that long ponytail hair and dresses like a substitute teacher, he's kind of cute. He's a yes, if there was a gun to my head. Where's my beer?

Bert, of course, pokes his head in, because I cannot possibly be alone for an entire minute. "Got to pee," he says. "Let's go soon." Then he says, "Why are you holding those?"

I hear the bathroom door close behind him in the hall.

It's just me and the balloons and passed out Bill, and even though I can't locate my beer I'm already having more fun back here than I was having in the front half of the house.

I want to tell Bill, it's not that I don't like them, people. I do. I've just never figured out how it all works. Is everyone faking it, like I've always suspected? Bill doesn't answer. Or are people really having a good time? Bill doesn't move. The good part, I guess, is when a person talks to a new person she's just met. Then she's not talking to the same old person she's always talking to.

Toilet flushing. Balloon ribbons in my hand. I sit down on the bed, on top of the coats and accidentally on Bill's left wrist. "Sorry," I say. Bill doesn't complain.

In college, I want to tell Bill, I'd be invited to parties and then drive to the location, drive slow down the street, turn around, and then drive by again. It was easy to tell which house was having the party, but I would pretend. I'd pretend I couldn't figure it out. And *too bad*, I'd tell myself, and then I'd drive home. Because at least then in the morning I could say I tried, that I found blah-blah street and drove up and down but couldn't find the right house, and that sucked, and I'm so sorry, and was the party fun. Isn't that better, I ask Bill. Isn't that better than not trying at all?

Out in the living room, people are singing *Happy Birthday dear Gerry*. I move my lips around the shape of the words.

There is the sound of the tap running, and then the bathroom door opens and Bert is back. He says, "Seriously. Why are you holding those?"

He says, "I'm missing the Simpsons right now."

I want to go. And I don't want to go. At home, everything will be the same.

Bert says, "I bet we'll try and sneak out and our car won't start. And then we'll have to come back into the party and ask somebody for a jump."

Bert pulls his black jacket from under passed out Bill's left hip.

He finds my purse and my coat underneath Bill's left foot.

And then Nan is standing in the doorway. She says, "You guys going through people's pockets back here?"

She sees me holding the balloons. She sees Bert in his jacket.

Bert says, "We're just going to slip out. Tell Gerry happy birthday."

And Nan says, "No. You tell him yourselves."

Then she says, "You can't have those balloons, you know. Those are Gerry's."

I wish we were already home.

"Okay," she says. "You can have the green one. Gerry hates green."

And this is when I notice my arms in the sleeves of my coat, husband at my side, balloon around my wrist. Already on our way. Back down the sidewalk, toward the car, toward the highway, to head home. Silence in the car except for the tires fast against asphalt, the balloon rubbing hollow against the roof, and the two of us breathing. We will not get lost. Him, driving. Me, sitting there.

THE ONLY ONE

It's not that I think my parents will get back together. But my friend Robin, her parents got a divorce and her dad lived in a motel next to a Mexican restaurant for a while and then her parents got undivorced and her dad moved back in. So it's possible. It happens.

Last week I did an oral report on waterfowl for science class. *Geese and ducks are grazers and need short green grass for food.* That was the first sentence. I got a B-, which pretty much sums up my life. A little better than average but nothing special. I learned that geese mate for life but not ducks. In the duck world there is a lot of weirdo hanky-panky stuff like corkscrew penises and forced copulation, which is basically duck rape, and even though everyone else in class laughed at that line, I didn't think it was funny at all.

Real human being sex, that's even more confusing. On that subject I know only three things. I know that my friend Tina and I used to play model. We'd lock the bathroom door and one of us would pose with our shirt pulled up and our pants pulled down while the other took fake pictures with an invisible camera. We'd act like we thought naked adult girls were supposed to act, which is like *Playboy* models: our chests arched up and shoulders thrown back. When one of us was finished posing, we'd switch. My pulse always raced, so I knew what we were doing was wrong but I didn't exactly know why. Afterwards, alone in my room, I'd bite my nails down to the quick.

I also know about kissing french. I did that with Eric Bingham in a closet at a party this summer. It was sort of gross and my tongue felt like a piece of meat that I was holding in my mouth at the same time I was trying to kiss someone and it made the kissing almost impossible. Kissing was on the way to sex and I knew that I wanted to know what sex was but I also knew I wasn't supposed to have sex because having sex would mean I was a slut and if I was slut everyone would want to have sex with me, and then I'd be stuck having sex with everybody all the time, which sounds exhausting. I don't know when I'd have time to practice the piano.

The last thing I know is that my boobs are getting big — bigger faster than other boobs around me, like the boobs themselves are aware of some competition I know nothing about. Amanda Klute is a grade above me and she has big boobs and all of us at Huntley Hills Middle School, the students, the teachers, even the janitor, we all know Amanda Klute has had sex already and her big boobs are like an advertisement for more. It's obvious my own big boobs mean trouble.

The only decent way to get out of class in middle school is to visit the guidance counselor's office. Before I stopped going, I used to see Miss Olson once a week which was as often as I could go without people suspecting I had real problems. I liked spending time in her office. It was different than every other part of the school. She had green spindly plants in ceramic pots sitting on top of the orange radiator under a long dirty window and it always smelled like peppermint gum. I liked being in there but I never told her much of anything. I never told her that I spent a lot of time imagining all the people who lived before me, the cave men and Spanish explorers and families in covered wagons and cowboys and Indians and Gold-rushers and hippies and yuppies, the whole of human history, imagining that all of them had probably had a lot of sex, and how that's so many people it seemed likely to me that there was no patch of land on this earth, except maybe parts of Mt. Everest and Antarctica, that hadn't been used by someone at some point to have sex with somebody else.

I never told Miss Olson how I'd stopped showering or about my mom saying I was starting to smell. I never told her that I thought about Mr. Casals, the dad of the two kids I babysit for, that I thought about my tongue in his mouth because maybe a man knew how to kiss without it being so gross and meat-like.

There is a boy my age who likes me. His name is Glen. He has a set of monster braces and plays the clarinet in band, not a great combination. I know he likes me because one time the phone rang when I was just home from school. I was listening to the microwave make my popcorn.

When I picked up, the phone said, "Sylvie. This is Glen Bell."

There was nothing to say so I didn't say anything back. But then he didn't say anything either. So finally I said, "What do you want?"

That's when he started singing that Stevie Wonder song. He sang, "*I just called to say I love you.*" It was beyond embarrassing. I thought I might die, right there, listening to Glen sing Stevie over the popping of microwave popcorn. He sang, "*I just called to say how much I care.*"

I hung up.

I'd first met Glen Bell a few weeks earlier at Mr. Pomfrey's annual Spring student piano recital. I was playing Clementi's Sonatina Op. 36 No. 3. Just that first page and a half through the main section to the first repeat and back again to the loud-quiet-big-deal ending. In my sheet music there are pencil marks all over in my seesaw crooked handwriting saying, *Practice this trouble area!* Saying, *For trill — 2 notes to every eighth.* Saying, to left hand, *Faster! Keep up!*

The tricky thing about the piece is that both hands start out in the treble clef for a bunch of bars and the two hands are doing totally different things but have to keep time with each other exactly. The left hand is like a metronome and the right hand is the one that gets to do all the fun stuff but can't fall behind.

Mr. Pomfrey teaches piano out of his house a few blocks from school. I walk there every Thursday afternoon, out of the Huntley Hills parking lot, past the first stop sign, over the wood bridge that crosses the creek, around the bend in the road and then up the steep driveway. During lessons he keeps an ashtray on the corner of the big grand piano so he can put down his always-burning cigarette in order to clap his hands to help remind me to keep time.

"BA-ba-BA-ba-BA-ba-BA," he says. "Four-four, Sylvie. This is not a waltz." His face is a mess of wrinkles and eyebrows and hairs sprouting from his pointy nose and these muddy brown spots he says are from the sun.

At the recital Glen Bell's little brother was playing *Go*

Tell Aunt Rhody and *Lightly Row* — the worst most boring songs ever but everyone has to play them that first year and then everyone in the audience claps like it's the performance of a lifetime.

After the recital when all the kids were milling around the refreshment table in their uncomfortable dress clothes, (*meaning*, Mr. Pomfrey says, *anything but jeans*,) this kid with a face full of metal and dark blue eyes came up to me. I recognized him as one of the 8th grade boys from school.

"I'm Glen Bell," he said. "Nice chops." He offered me his hand to shake. I didn't shake it. He was obviously a weirdo. "I should know," he said. "I'm a musician too."

We both stared at the refreshment table and I reached for one of the chocolate chip cookies on the dessert tray, but my mom saw from across the room where she was talking to Mrs. Pomfrey and stared her eyes into mine like I'm watching you, so I moved my hand over to the carrot and celery stick tray and grabbed a few of those instead.

Glen said, "I play clarinet." He was wearing a suit and tie which seemed like overdoing it to me since he wasn't even playing in the recital, his brother was.

I said, "I know. You're in band." My mom's back was turned for a second so I grabbed a cracker with cheese whiz on the top.

"Yeah, jazz band too," he said. "You ever seen us?"

I didn't want to talk with cracker in my mouth so I shook my head no, but of course I'd seen them. The whole school was forced to sit through a set of their squawking at the mandatory assemblies before winter and summer breaks. As if band isn't bad enough, a kid's got to go and further muck up his prospects at life by playing in the school jazz band, a group with the unfortunate name of *Take the H Train* which I think was supposed to be some kind of reference to the H in Huntley Hills but really, everyone said, just seemed like encouragement to use heroin.

"We have a piano at our house, for my brother," Glen said.

"Yeah," I said. "We have one too." It was like talking to a houseplant. "That's how I practice."

"No," he said. "I mean you could come over sometime and you could play piano and I could play clarinet." His hand reached across the refreshment table and grabbed a chocolate chip cookie and handed it to me. "You're good enough. I don't always like to play with other people because most people can't keep up with me. But we could really, you know, jam."

When I didn't say anything he said, "I think we'd make beautiful music together."

When I didn't say anything he said, "That was supposed to be a joke. Anyway, bye."

After Glen walked off and I finished almost dying I somehow got stuck talking to Laura Schmeigel's grandfather who smelled like menthol rub and I kept trying to figure how to eat that chocolate chip cookie without my mom seeing.

Later at home I thought about my tongue in Glen Bell's mouth. I wasn't sure how well it would fit in there with all that metal or if maybe my lips would get all cut up. All I knew was that everything would be dark because my eyes would be closed because that's how people kiss which doesn't make any sense. If I ever get my tongue into someone else's mouth again I'm going to keep my eyes open and see what the whole deal looks like.

After my mom and dad got divorced my dad moved to San Diego, which is only a six-hour car ride, my mom keeps saying, but might as well be about a million miles away. He has an apartment with a pull-out sofa all ready for me when I come to visit and there's a balcony that "If you stand on your tiptoes," he wrote once in a postcard, "you can see the ocean."

I get postcards from my dad every week. He's always asking me to write back, but that seems so weird — to write to your own dad to tell him about your life that he should just know about because he should be living with you because he's your dad. He wouldn't want the postcards I would send anyway. He doesn't want to know about Mom working a lot and being so tired she drinks wine and doesn't remember stuff we talked about the next morning. He doesn't want to know about me wanting my tongue down Glen Bell's throat or wishing Mr. Casals would walk me home and tell me I look pretty.

I was watching MTV when Glen called the second time. When the phone rang, I answered it.

Glen said, "It's Glen Bell."

I didn't say anything.

Glen said, "Do you want to go on a date with me?"

I said, "I'm not allowed to date."

Glen said, "What about a movie? That's not a date."

I said, "That's a date."

Glen said, "Not really. It's more just a movie."

I said, "Maybe. Would we have to be alone?"

Glen said, "I guess not. I could bring my little brother."

On the television, a video I'd seen a thousand times was playing: a shirtless guy danced around a snowy forest.

I said, "Okay. But don't tell my mom."

He said, "I won't."

. . .

My mom pulled the accordion nozzle out from a box of wine, me and her in the kitchen. Her clothes were always tired layers of crumpled fabric by the end of each day, her blouse untucked from the skirt of her suit, her matching blazer hung over the arms of a kitchen chair. It was late, way past dark, and I hadn't yet microwaved my Lean Cuisine for dinner. My arm was on the open freezer door and I was letting all the cold air out. I was trying to decide between Chicken Cordon Bleu or Beef Lasagna. What I wanted was a cheeseburger and onion rings and fries but my mom says we can't eat like that because our genes make it easy for women in our family to be fat.

"Can I go to a movie this weekend," I asked.

"With whom?" Her lips curled around the m in whom. Her wine glass rang as she set it back on the kitchen counter.

"With a friend. Two friends. The Bells." Technically this was not a lie.

She was midway through a box of wine so when she spoke it was with her eyes half-closed and her lips half-smiled.

She said, "I don't know the Bells. Who are the Bells?" Her speech was slow. She was very tired and a little drunk. Or vice versa.

"They're from Mr. Pomfrey's. They were at the recital."

"Those sisters who played the duet?" she said. "Oh, weren't they wonderful. Why don't you ever play any-thing like that?"

"I don't have a sister," I said.

My hand reached for the box of Beef Lasagna. "So can I go?"

When she didn't answer I saw that she'd gone back to

falling asleep while reading a magazine while watching TV.

Technically this wasn't a no.

I heard my mom on the phone with my dad. They were planning my trip to see him when school's out for summer in a few weeks. *Well, you can't let her eat whatever she wants. You know how she puts on weight. I know you're her father. I know that. Well that's your choice. It's none of your business. I'm not answering that.* When they were done she called me to the phone from my room saying, "Your father wants to talk to you." The word father out of her mouth like spitting out a bug.

I was supposed to meet Glen Bell outside by the ticket booth at one o'clock. All week I kept thinking I'd get up the nerve to tell my mom I had a date that wasn't really a date that was just a movie but I knew she'd say no so I never said anything. Then somehow it was one-fifteen and my mom was driving me to the nursery so she could buy dirt for some new project she had going in the backyard and I realized I'd just stood up the only boy who'd ever asked me out.

Why adults pay perfectly good money for dirt is one of those things I will never understand.

"Soil," she said. "Not dirt."

"It's dirt," I said. "It's free. It's everywhere."

I pictured Glen Bell with his little brother waiting at the movie theater. How long would he wait? Would he go to the movie without me? Would he just go home? I got an icky feeling in my stomach. At a stoplight I thought about jumping out and running to the movie theater, but

I'm kind of a slow runner. My mom would've definitely caught up to me in her car. Plus my most defining trait is that I'm not very brave, so I never would have done it anyway. If I were more brave maybe I would've just told my mom the truth and demanded she allow me to meet Glen for a movie. If I were more brave, maybe I would've said that I knew Dad left because she told him to. That I knew she made the choice for all of us.

The last time I saw Miss Olson, she basically told me that I smelled. She was smiling at me from behind her desk in front of the orange radiator with the spindly plants, everything smelling like peppermint gum. She said the growing body goes through a lot of changes and, "I'm sure you've noticed that as a body changes, its smells change too."

Even though I knew then that I hated her and wouldn't ever talk to her again, I knew it was true. I smelled different. I'd noticed it. Humid. Musty. Like I needed to be put out on a clothesline to dry.

I sat across from her in a beige plastic chair and nodded my head like she was imparting the wisdom of the centuries, but I would never tell her the truth. The truth was that I just got bored. The same thing everyday. Soap all over my body. That orange bar of Dial on my washcloth. And how it smelled like aftershave or something, that soap. Like Dad. Also because gross stuff was happening. Hair was starting to grow in my armpits. My mom was urging me to shave my legs. I was obviously becoming a man. Or an ape. No, I wasn't about to tell Miss Olson anything at all.

When my parents split up it was a good thing I saw it

coming because neither of them ever bothered to talk to me about it. They figured that when Dad didn't come home from his business meeting and started writing me postcards about his new apartment I'd put together the fact that we weren't really a family anymore.

A few months after he was gone, my mom got all I Am Woman Hear Me Roar and changed her name back to what it was before she was married. She said it was fine for me to keep Dad's name so now her name is different from mine. If our two names were next to each other on a piece of paper, there'd be no way to know she was my mother and I was her daughter. It would just look like two totally different people's names coincidentally near each other. The names of two strangers.

I called Glen the day after I stood him up.

I said, "Are you mad?"

He said, "I'm mad."

I said, "I'm sorry. I told you I couldn't go on a date."

He said, "I'm never talking to you again."

A bird with greenish black shiny feathers flew up to the feeder my mom had hanging from an eave outside the kitchen window. It pecked its bird head into the food opening a few times and then flew away.

"This is kind of a weird question," I said. "Do you take showers or baths?"

"I like where this is going," he said.

"Shut up," I said. "I told you it was weird."

"Usually showers. Sometimes baths," he said. "Why?"

On the other side of the window the bird flew back and brought a friend with him this time. Two of them pecking their beaks into the feeder, some seeds falling from their mouths, their heads swiveling back and forth as they chewed.

I said, "I haven't really felt much like showering lately."

"So you're more into baths?" he said.

"No, I haven't really felt like those either."

If I ever wrote a postcard to Glen Bell I'd write: "Dear Glen, It's okay if you want to touch my boobs. It's not your fault. I'm sorry if I smell bad. You should know I might be turning into a man. ~~Love, Sylvie.~~ Sincerely, Sylvie."

I'm not sure what happened. I know that one time I was doing homework in the kitchen and I watched my mom put on her apron, chop vegetables and cook a roast, shout out that dinner was ready, put the veggies and roast onto three plates, hand one to me and one to my dad, take her apron off, sit down at her place at the table, take a sip of wine, then stand up, take Dad's plate from him as he was cutting the meat, and scrape every bit of his food into the sink without ever saying a word until he said her name once. *Clara.* Then she screamed at him. Screamed *jackass* and *bastard* and *arrogant.* I took my plate into the den and turned on the television loud. We never ate at the kitchen table again. Even now that Dad's gone, we still don't. I eat in front of an open book on the floor of the den. Mom eats standing up in the kitchen in front of the TV.

If I ever wrote a postcard to my mom I would write: "Dear Mom, I don't like it here anymore. I hate eating frozen diet food. When I visit Dad, first thing, I'm going to get a cheeseburger and onion rings. I'm going to dip the onion rings in mayonnaise. Love, Sylvie."

I call Glen.

"What's it like having a brother?" I say.

"Annoying," he says.

"No really," I say.

"It is. It's annoying."

"But he's always around, right?" I say.

"Oh my god, yes. He's *always* around," he says. "He was even around on the date I was supposed to take you on."

"You said it wasn't a date," I say. "I feel really bad about that."

"Yeah," he says. "You should."

When I don't say anything he says, "What are you doing right now?"

I'm watching TV with the sound off. It's a commercial for chips.

"Nothing," I say.

"It must be so awesome being the only one," he says.

On the TV, cheesy nacho chips dance their way out of a chip bag into a kid's mouth.

"I guess so," I say.

I can hear far off piano music coming through the phone from Glen's side.

"Do you only like me because of my boobs?" I say.

"What?" he says.

"Nothing," I say.

Even if Glen really likes me it's easy to see how it will be. He'll want to touch my boobs and then he'll want to have sex with me and then he'll tell his friends and they'll want to touch my boobs and then I'll be one of those girls whose boobs are touched and has sex with boys, and I'll never know if anyone really likes me, *me*, ever again.

"Do you think my parents will ever get back together?" I say.

"Sylvie," he says.

"Tell me," I say.

On TV, the commercials are over and a video plays, the sound still off.

"No," he says. "That doesn't really happen."

"Glen Bell," I say.

"Yes?" he says.

A woman in a tight dress and super high heels stands in place and moves her hips.

"Nothing."

YES

Chuck rings the doorbell and I have my luggage all ready set go by the front door but when I let him in, instead of reaching for my suitcase, Chuck kneels on the hard tile in the entryway and says will you marry me and so I say all right: Chuck's mom Gladys is watching the whole thing from her car right out front, engine idling, window rolled down, extra long cigarette burning between two straight fingers. After that I yell goodbye to my dad who says bye back but doesn't come out of the garage to say it, then Chuck helps me squeeze my suitcase and backpack into the crammed trunk of his mom's car and slam the lid shut. And we're off.

So now I'm engaged. I am reserved, like a table at a restaurant. The ring is the kind of ring it's supposed to be — yellow gold, small white diamond, princess cut. For a moment sunlight shines through the Honda's rear window and hits the tidy rock, refracting into a rainbow of color and I feel a warm smooth stone in my center and think, *Look at me.*

Gladys catches my eye in the rearview and smiles. She says, "Congratulations, Honey."

Her teeth are yellowed and there are wrinkle lines around her puckered mouth as she drags off her first cigarette of the trip. Married, I think, that's something to be.

. . .

The blue interior of Gladys' Honda Accord is soft and plush and spotless except for the reek of cigarette smoke and the tiny burn holes from flying ash in the backseat. Above me, a big orange trunk is strapped to the top of the roof rack along with two black duffel bags that are held down by bungee cords and a cardboard box that says SHOES in black magic marker. When we really get going on the freeway, the weight on top rocks the car side to side, like we are on boat.

I bet we look like a family, the three of us, me the younger sibling in the back. But I'm a fiancée now, two e's. I am not just a daughter anymore.

It is a long drive to Boston and we are going by the north. The north! I roll down my window in the backseat to get some fresh air, the cool against my bare arms, freeway wind loud in my ear whipping my long hair into a mess. I am seventeen and it is summer and I am free and also Chuck's mother is driving so not that free.

I can smell the burn of paper and tobacco as Gladys brings the red-hot ring of the car lighter to the cigarette pursed between her lips. Gladys smokes like it was just invented, brand new and full of possibility. When we drive into the heat of the day she smokes with the windows rolled up and the air conditioner on high. She has a leather cigarette wallet with a metal snap, like a coin purse but longer. It is always around. Along with everything else, there are two cartons of Winston Light 100s in the trunk.

When Chuck and I met at his friend's keg party, he told me he loved me first thing. I was in the beer line with my blue plastic cup and I said, *too bad, I don't date men only*

42

boys. And he said, *don't worry because I'm not that grown up.*
He'd just been dumped by his first fiancée and I was in my
last year of high school. After dating for most of the
school year Chuck said we should take a road trip and I
said, *yes, yes, yes,* I'd always wanted to take a road trip and
pictured the two of us on his bike riding desolate roads
through small towns and deserts and Chuck said, *perfect,*
it's settled, my mom's moving to Massachusetts and she needs
help driving her stuff out — so here we are.

When we start to gain elevation on our way over the
Sierra Nevadas, Gladys wants me to tell the story again.

"What were you thinking?" she says.

She probably doesn't want me to answer that honestly.
My lightning fast ferris wheel of thoughts was — *what are*
you doing? No, don't kneel. Oh god, please don't be proposing.
Okay, you're proposing. This is so awkward. I will do anything
to get you back up on your feet so this moment can be over and
we can go back quick to how things were before. Also, I was
thinking about how Chuck has been engaged before. I
tried to imagine the time before this one when he knelt
down for another woman he was willing to marry. Within
a year Chuck found two of us, which demonstrated that
Chuck had really good fortune or far too broad criteria for
a good wife.

Reno is the first stop on the way to Boston. We get a
smoking room at a motor lodge shaped like an L, its name
in neon lights. There are two double beds with impossibly
ugly flowered polyester bedspreads: Chuck and I are in the
bed by the door and his mother is in the one by the
bathroom. Staying in a room two doors down is a husky

stubble-headed fellow wearing a black leather jacket despite the heat that says Hells Angels Sacramento on the back. His sloped metal monster parked in the spot out front. Chuck's face releases a huge grin.

"Cool," he says.

"Aren't they kind of like a racist gang," I say.

"I meant the bike," Chuck says.

Chuck's got an older model Kawasaki, 750 CCs. Back at home when we are having a good day or when I am having a bad one he takes us out. People stare. We ride down the canyon, over the hill, past the farms, out towards the sea and by the time we get there my hair is all whipped in little knots and my cheeks are red and I feel such love for him that I ache.

Everything, everybody, all of us, we smell like cigarettes. We take showers in turn, a small low tub with a metal nozzle that spits water out with such force it stings my naked skin. The nozzle sticks out of the shower wall at shoulder height so I have to bend my knees and lean backwards into the spray to get my hair wet. Chuck and his mom are a couple inches shorter than me and in the cramped fiberglass stall I resent them for it.

As soon as we're clean, we get back in the car. We head down 4th Street and cruise through downtown. Reno is a smudge of tallish buildings and neon-signed casinos, dry desert mountains all around. It's almost a tiny Vegas but feels unfinished, like someone took a lunch break in the middle of building it and never came back.

Gladys takes us to a casino she had been to twenty years ago because she remembers liking their buffet. The place is all white tile floors and pineapple on ice. It is heat-lamped islands of gloppy gravy and knifed overdone roast

omah County Library
that you checked out:

People like you : stories
D: 31168116572239
due: 3/14/2020,23:59

checkouts for session:1
checkouts:2

omah County Library
88.5123
lib.org
s Anything!

on humid silver trays. I eat scalloped potatoes and a baked potato and two white rolls with lots of butter and chocolate pudding for dessert. I drink four refills of root beer.

Gladys says, "I'm bushed." She pulls a cigarette from her little coin purse and lights it with a clear plastic lighter she keeps tucked into the little purse's front pocket.

She says, "I'm going to head in and play a few slots." She motions toward the main casino room. "Then drive back to the motel." Smoke in. Smoke out. "You two okay to walk?"

As soon as his mom disappears into the dark mouth of the casino Chuck asks to see my finger. I straighten and wiggle the five fingers on my left hand so he can see the sparkle jump in the light. I've only been wearing the ring for ten hours but already he's checked on it three times.

He says, "I love seeing it on you."

We set off from the buffet entrance through the main lobby and toward the slots. Chuck is legal, he's twenty-three, and I am not so I lean into him and smile, hide my face in my hair, like I'm older and laughing at a funny joke, and I make certain that people passing can get a glimpse of the ring. It helps. A diamond can do that. Make a woman out of a girl.

Chuck sits me down at a slot machine with two rolls of nickels and then he heads to a blackjack table in the middle of the noisy flashing dim room. I sit by myself and sink one whole roll of nickels before a bare-shouldered waitress walks by in a burgundy nylon wraparound skirt. Her face gives away the age of her body.

"A Bud," I say.

I know to only order bottled beer in a casino because they water down the hard stuff. The waitress plays along and doesn't card me. I know to tip.

Around me are sounds of the singing machines and the

metal meeting metal meeting plastic of coins into a bucket. I look around for Gladys, it'd be nice to sit with someone, but I don't see her. I wonder if this is what it is like to be married, alone and obligated all at once.

Before I finish that first beer I'm out of nickels and bored beyond belief. I slalom through the slots and game tables and find Chuck sitting next to an older fellow with a long face and gaunt cheeks. Both men, their eyes deep into the set of two cards in their hands. I hover behind them and watch. Chuck has a red seven on the green felt next to a good size pile of red and white and yellow chips. An empty shot glass on the felt next to a brown bottle of beer sweating in the light. He wins the hand and then I touch his shoulder.

"A few more hands," he says. "I'm winning! I'll come get you." He hands me a yellow chip. "Go get some more nickels."

Be patient. Keep busy. When he's ready, he'll come get me. And isn't this like every Brontë sisters book I've ever read — the younger woman waiting for the older man to rescue her. Waiting to be saved, those girls. Always waiting.

The security guard that kicks me out is barely older than me. His uniform, dark pants and a dark short-sleeve collared shirt, is so new I can see the creases in the fabric where it was folded up to fit the packaging. After he asks for my ID and I say nothing, he doesn't say much. He doesn't need to. We both know why I'm getting the boot.

The dark glass doors close behind us and we are out on the sidewalk in the warm well-lit night of Reno and when he takes his hand away from the small of my back I register the absence of heat. He looks behind him and then looks at my face and his shoulders relax a tiny bit. His black hair is cut too short for his round face, making him look like a small serious boy.

"Thanks for making that so easy," he says.

He looks down at the ground, bends onto a knee to tie his untied bootlace.

Life sounds on the street, high heels on pavement, a woman's laugh, engine idling at the light, a car door slamming shut, and always the bright on-off flash of neon overhead.

"My boyfriend's inside," I say. "Fiancé," I say.

"I can't let you back in there," he says. He switches legs and double knots the other boot's laces.

"That's okay. Do you want to see the ring?" I say.

He stands up and looks at my hand, fingers wiggling to catch the light.

"We're driving across the country with his mom," I say. "It's kind of weird really."

"Yeah. I'd want to be alone with you if we were engaged," he says.

He looks down at his boots again. Checks the walkie talkie on his belt.

"Thanks," I say. "That's nice."

A police car speeds by us, lights flashing but no siren.

"What kind of ring would you've bought me?" I say.

Another police car speeds past. His eyes follow the sound down the street. He clears his throat.

"Anyway, even if you're married, you can't be in there unless you're twenty-one. And you're not, right?"

"Not married. Just engaged," I say. "Some people are engaged for a long time. It could be a few years before we do anything like that."

The muscles in his face gather into a serious expression. "Got to get back," he says. He points at my hand.

"Good luck with all that." And then walks away from me, back inside.

I sit on the curb. The ground is still warm from the day's sun. Cars drive back and forth in the street, headlights, taillights, exhaust. A man in cowboy boots stumbles along the sidewalk across the street, shirt untucked from his jeans. A friend walks next to him, his arm around the cowboy's back, holding him up, moving him forward.

My thumb plays with the ring, slipping it back and forth along the skin of my finger with ease. I toy with it until it falls to the cement and sings a hollow clang. It lands on the sidewalk next to a smudge of gummy residue and a squashed red-lipped cigarette butt. It's a good feeling to know that someone is willing to marry you.

I do not feel like waiting to be rescued tonight so I head back up 4th Street to the motel. I never worry that I'll get lost. I am a master at finding my way somewhere I've been before, even if I've only been there once.

I sit on the hood of Gladys' car across from the nook that houses the motel's vending machines. A dumping crash as new ice chips are made and dropped into the refrigerated belly with the other ice. The overloud canned laughter of a sitcom seeps out of the open motel office door.

Chuck will find his way back to me soon. He'll figure out I left and head back to the motel. Find me on the hood of the car and kiss me with his warm beer and whiskey breath, tell me about his winning or losing streak. I won't tell him about the security guard. That's just for me. He'll be so drunk he will forget to ask about the ring. We'll probably sneak quiet into the room where Gladys will be asleep with the TV on and then Chuck and I will squabble about whether or not to have sex a few feet from his sleeping mother until I cave and agree and we'll have missionary position sex with the covers pulled up over our heads and I won't come (I never will with him).

Here he is now.

I wake up later thinking it is morning but it is still night. The television is off and the room is dark except for a ribbon of streetlight bright in my face through the crack in the curtains. My naked legs are tangled up with Chuck's. The air in the room is heavy with old cigarette smoke and the stale night breathing of three people and I am thirsty, so thirsty, but I don't get up. My worry about Chuck isn't that there might be a better man out there for me. The world is filled with better and worse men. It's not that. It's that what if I decide after the fact that I don't want to be married to anyone at all.

If I could propose, what I'd want to marry is that feeling I feel when Chuck and I are riding fast on his bike, winding our way up the forested incline, our bodies intuitively leaning left and right with the weight of the beautiful machinery underneath us, the two-lane road all ours except for the passing of the occasional car headed in the opposite direction and oh how we feel sorry for them, those passengers, they do not know what they're missing, the warm air against my bare shoulders, the streams of sunlight sneaking through the heavy pines, the smell of dusty heat and warmed pavement and the cool damp of the forest floor, my arms wrapped around Chuck, my smile so wide I have to tuck my face into his shoulder so I don't swallow air, my whole body, each cell, singing with the abandon of being part of every single thing.

Who needs a wedding when I've known a thing like that.

I can't go back to sleep now. Nothing to do but wait. If I wait long enough time will catch up. The streetlight shuts off. The sun hides behind the northern Nevada mountains before peeking over the steep ridge and Gladys wakes to light her first cigarette of the day. Chuck will wake up any minute now and ask to see the ring on my finger. He will look for it on the nightstand. He will want to know where it is. How can I tell him. How do I tell him it never occurred to me that I could say no.

THE THINGS WE KNOW NOTHING ABOUT

I went to the burrito place, like I always went to the burrito place, the one in our old neighborhood, the one with the long lines of people waiting to order and the colored bulbs strung across the patio and the upside down neon sombreros hanging from the ceiling. Our new neighborhood didn't have a place to order a burrito. Our new neighborhood had bored kids and no sidewalks and stop signs that nobody stopped at. Our new neighborhood was two blocks from 82nd Avenue, a busy thoroughfare of big box stores and mini-malls and giant coffee chains with crappy coffee. Also there were hookers.

In the old neighborhood, it was bikes in the front yards and hellos on the sidewalks and big trees shading the streets. I was finding it difficult to forget. That's why I went back to the old neighborhood and walked into the burrito place and waited in the long line to order my veggie burrito with extra sour cream. I was pregnant and depressed and I thought a burrito might do the trick. What I wanted was for everything to go back to how it was before.

The guy who's always there behind the counter, the one with big eyebrows and the radish tattooed on his forearm, he still recognized me.

His smile was all teeth.

He said, "Hey, it's been a while."

"Yes," I said. I was debating whether to tell him I was

pregnant. I didn't know him at all. He was just the burrito guy.

He asked what he always asked. He said, "The usual? For here?"

And without thinking, I said what I always used to say. "Yes," I said. "Okay."

I paid. He gave me an order number. No. 29. I sat down at the counter and that's when he brought me the bottle of beer.

"Cheers," he said. He went back to the register.

He was right. I did always order this beer with my burrito. I didn't want to offend him by giving it back. He'd remembered everything and I hated offending people. My inside voice said, just shut your trap and sit with the beer. No need to drink it. Bottle's already open and paid for. Don't make trouble.

It had been a week since I'd had any morning sickness. On my small wooden stool, arms on the counter, I tried to look natural sitting next to that beer. Nobody knew anything. I tried it out in my hand. Cap off, cold glass against my palm, the familiar weight of twelve ounces. A few sips couldn't hurt. It was just one beer. It was just a brain making a decision for a body.

I brought the bottle to my lips. I waited to be struck by lightning.

"Number twenty nine," said the burrito guy. He slid my food across the counter and took my number. "Enjoy," he said.

It seemed like a sign. Also, I am not one to waste a drink, a habit inherited from my mother-in-law, so I drank it.

Afterwards, I drove home to the new neighborhood. The streetlights were just coming on, overlapping with the sunset in my rearview mirror. My window was down, the radio off. The only sound was the sound of the engine and the other cars as they passed me going one direction or another. I flowed with the flow of traffic. I felt right side up. Good day sunshine. At last, here was the me I'd been waiting for.

So I did it again the next week.

And again, the week after that.

And then I kept doing it.

All that summer, week after week, it was my secret indulgence. Exhilarating, private, all mine. Back to the old neighborhood, order a burrito, drink a beer while I wait. Then, cinnamon gum on the long drive home to the unstopping stop signs and the hookers and Staffy, my husband of two springs and one summer.

Staffy has a small penis but he loves me and he married me and also he supports my art. I dabble in ceramics, occasionally selling some pieces at arts and crafts fairs on the West Coast. I'm not very good. But I really love glazing. So I stick with it. I feel the same way about Staffy. I'm no fool. I know what else is out there. Staffy may have some imperfections, the anxiety, the cologne, the nail biting, but the being married part is fun to tell people. So I stick with it.

I was trying to have the same attitude about the baby. But even then I knew that when the whole thing was over, when this baby was finally born in five months, or twenty two weeks, or one hundred and fifty four days, I'd be having a lot less fun than the fun I wasn't having already.

At my first appointment, I'd refused the initial ultrasound, and settled instead on the Doppler thingy that can hear the heartbeat. Hearing was enough. I wasn't ready to see anything yet. I needed more time. Staffy, on the other hand, couldn't contain himself about the baby. His hands always on my barely-showing belly. Palm to my navel. Sometimes I loved this, the best we ever were. Other times, I wished I could disappear until the baby was born.

That was the thing about the beer — once I made it through the first few nauseating sips, I'm sure I became a much better person, courageous, patient, kind; everything you could want in a mother. Also, beer has hops. Hops are grains. And grains are healthy. Grains are good for you. Grains are recommended by the Surgeon General.

The hedges were tall, as tall as a person standing on another person's shoulders. And they were wide, as wide as a city sidewalk. They separated our backyard in the new neighborhood from the street. We'd never trimmed them and they were out of control, so thick nobody on one side would ever see what anybody on the other side was up to. It was the perfect place to be alone.

Until I realized I wasn't.

The first time I understood what the hookers were doing on the street side of our hedges was the Tuesday after the week after Labor Day. And Tuesday was trash night. I loved trash night because trash night was the night before burrito night. On burrito night, I could do whatever I wanted. Like a contract had been formed between me and the universe. And I was allowed to drink once a week, and the universe was allowed to let me have a normal baby. It was pretty simple. Really, it's the least the universe could do, having left me in this crappy neighborhood, all pregnant and married and alone.

Staffy was bending over our bins. He was militant about separating the recycling. So careful about the smallest things. He really would make a wonderful father. Or maybe not. Maybe attention to detail makes for a terrible father. What do I know.

Staffy was on the lip of our driveway, where it meets the street, where our trashcan waits on trash night, right next to the hedges. Staffy stopped sorting and pointed out a tiny beat-up Honda hatchback from the 70s, white and rusted, parked a few feet away, on the street side of the hedges. The Honda hatchback was bouncing. And even though it was overcast and night was on its way, I could see from the streetlight that there was a woman straddling a man in the driver's seat. A woman, facing us, bouncing up and down on the driver, facing away.

I said, "Are you fucking kidding me?"

I started to walk to the car. I had my hand on my belly, and even though it was almost impossible to tell I was pregnant then, I was prepared to play it up. Strangers! Having sex! By a pregnant woman's hedges!

But Staffy grabbed my arm. "Don't bother them."

The beat up little Honda bouncing.

He said, "They might have weapons."

I said, "They're hookers, Staffy. Not assassins."

Still, I decided to yell instead.

I yelled the only thing I could think of. "Hey!"

The bouncing stopped.

I yelled again. "Hey!"

And then the woman climbed off the man in the driver's seat and the man started up the hatchback. They drove off, the little car weaving left and right before settling on straight. We finished putting the trash and recycling out, but I felt sort of sick. Even with the life I've lived and what I know, it was kind of disturbing. It made me wonder about all the things that are going on around us all the time, the things we know nothing about.

.   .   .

By our house in our new neighborhood, next to the café and the sports bar and the auto body shop, there is a business called Stumptown Tub N' Tan. It's a nondescript storefront, by which I mean it's a storefront that I drive by and never pay attention to. A person driving by might think, there is a business where I can go to get a tub or a tan, and then that person will probably keep driving because who really does either of those things, especially both, and at the same place. And then, after living in our new neighborhood, it occurs to me: the hookers. The hookers are the ones that tub n' tan.

When I told Staffy, he said, "Yes. You're probably right."

He said, "But I bet the hookers tan on their own time. And the tubs, well, I bet they're on the clock."

For a minute we said nothing. Mental image of a woman, naked and skinny with stretchmarks and scars, slipping a leg into a hot tub — sharp smell of chlorine, jets on high — and a hairy middle-aged man in the water staring at her sagging breasts and whacking off.

I said to Staffy, "I wonder how often they change the water."

At our monthly two-person, ladies-only brunch, Staffy's mom told the waiter she wanted a Bloody Mary, and when the waiter's big bald head turned toward me, I put my thinking face on: I thought of water, and juice, and beer, and scotch. I made eye contact, nothing to hide. I opened my mouth, and my mouth told the waiter's big bald head I wanted the house chardonnay. Wine, after all, seemed more civilized. Because wine is only grapes, which are fruit. And fruit is natural. Fruit is good for you. Fruit is recommended by the Surgeon General.

We sat at a table on a sunny patio, ivy growing on the wall, smell of coffee and potatoes and the fresh tar a crew was using to repave the street in front of the restaurant. My sense of smell these days was keen. Staffy's mom, Vicky, waved a hand in front of her face, big gold ring, long nails painted red, then she brought the straw to her mouth and sipped, removed the celery stalk and took a crunch.

She said, "Del, I drank plenty when I was pregnant with Staffy."

The tar fumes and the heavy loud clatter of metal meeting rock from the street crew made it hard to pay attention.

She crunched again and sipped and said, "We didn't know anything then."

The stem of my glass of chardonnay was in my hand so I swallowed a healthy serving. I said, "My doctor said a drink or two was fine."

And I took another sip.

We sat across from each other and I listened to Vicky choke that stalk of celery down. I ate a breadstick from the bread basket. I hated these lunches. When Vicky got up to pee I ordered a second chardonnay. No way I'd get caught: Vicky never looked over the checks when she paid and she always took forever in the bathroom. I had plenty of time to polish off that first glass and put my empty on the table behind me. I knew her routine, face powder, lipstick, brush through her hair. What was the point of it? Death was coming anyway.

She took so long I could have ordered a third but I didn't want to seem like a hog.

My Eggs Florentine arrived at the same time Vicky came back from the bathroom. She ordered another Bloody Mary.

The big bald waiter asked if I needed another drink. "No," I said. "One is enough."

After dropping Vicky off at her condo, I went home and sat on our cement front steps, the tiny buzz from lunch hovering around me. A woman my age walked by, pushing a baby stroller in the street, since, like I said, the new neighborhood didn't have many sidewalks. I felt sorry for her, pushing a blanketed lump in a stroller in the middle of the day. I thought about me pushing a lump around in the middle of the day. I wondered if I would love the lump. If the lady walking by loved her lump too. The big arrival was only four months away, one season in a year, and then it would just be here. All the time. Part of me. Forever. The just me days I still had left were loud in my ear. I did my best to honor them. If the baby disliked the occasional beverage, it would be sure to let me know. But it never made a peep. In fact the baby didn't move around much at all.

Summer crept off. The arts and crafts fairs mostly over by now, and I'd done nothing this year. Already what I loved was slipping away. Autumn snuck in and it was my birthday and for the occasion Staffy made a pot pie.

"Yum," he said. "Pot pie." He pointed at his plate with his fork. "From scratch."

Between bites I nodded and mumbled approval, thinking how much better this meal would be with a nice big bottle of red wine.

Staffy wiped at the corners of his mouth with a paper napkin. He sat up straighter, shoulders back. He must have read my mind.

"I've decided," he said. "I've had about enough."

The jig was up. He knew about the booze. About me

not loving the neighborhood. Me not loving the baby.
He'd tell me he was angry and disappointed. Maybe he'd
ask me to leave. I'd pretend to want to stay. I'd say some
sorry things. And then I'd run upstairs and pack a bag and
drive back to rent a room in the old neighborhood, where
I could push my soon-to-be blanketed lump around on
sidewalks, under a canopy of trees, on my way to buy a
burrito.

He said, "I found more condoms in the gutter."

Staffy was talking about the hookers.

"And this morning," he said. He took a bite of pot pie.
"Inside-out latex gloves."

His mouth chewed. He said, "What are those for?"

I had some ideas.

He said, "I don't want to know."

I watched him eat, slow, circular chews, his mouth
slightly open, his eyes on my eyes. I knew him well
enough to know he was waiting for a response. I just
didn't know him well enough to know which one.

Finally I heard him swallow. I tried to think of something to say, but I thought instead of how today was my
birthday and something like that only happens once a
year, and that I should probably allow myself one drink
tonight.

Staffy sighed a heavy sigh, breath through his tight lips
from deep inside, wiped at his mouth again with that napkin, pushed his chair back, and walked to the coat closet.
When he walked back he had a box in his arms, a box the
size of a toaster oven covered in shiny giftwrap and a big
gold bow.

He moved my plate out of the way even though I
hadn't finished yet, set the shiny box on my placemat next
to a fallen wet chunk of pot pie.

"Happy birthday," he said.

It just sat there, that wet chunk, right next to my birthday present.

A whiff of Staffy's cologne just then made me sick to my stomach. I wiped my hands on the napkin in my lap: my thighs, I'd noticed, already getting bigger.

"Open it," he said.

The shiny box in front of me, I thought of all the things it could be. The possibility every present holds. I thought maybe a new glaze for my pots. Bigger pants for my widening thighs. A new spatula. And then I opened it.

I said, "Thank you." But I didn't understand what I was seeing.

Staffy said, "It's a Wexby Industrial Super Search Eye Spotlight."

He said, "It's ten million candlepower."

I stared at the handheld portable spotlight.

"It's for the hookers," he said. "I charged it up yesterday."

My half-eaten pot pie stared up at me.

He said, "Let's try it out."

The backyard was pitch black, couldn't find the moon, and I didn't want to trip. So I thought I'd point my new Super Search Eye Spotlight at the ground like a flashlight. But when I clicked it on, the light was ferocious. It swallowed up the dark, a superhuman ray, a perfect straight beam, like a mobile sun I controlled. I loved it.

We waited for a while on our side of the hedges, what a birthday, but nothing happened. Staffy seemed disappointed, so I said, "Let's do a dry run."

"Good idea," he said.

Staffy played the hooker. I played myself.

We did a couple drills in the backyard. Staffy kneeled on the grass and said, "Okay, I'm fellating someone now."

Then I shined the bright light on his face to bust him.

Poor Staffy looked pasty in that monster light, and guilty, so guilty. I guess that was the idea.

After two practice rounds, finally I said what I was really thinking: "Is there cake?"

He was holding his hand up in front of his face. "Anyway," Staffy said, "I can't see so well right now."

There was a cake. Chocolate, my favorite, with vanilla icing. And in the middle of the cake was a candle, one perfect birthday candle waiting to be lit. But Staffy said his pupils hurt. He was worried he'd almost gone blind.

He said, "I'm going to bed." Staffy had his defeated voice on. I felt bad about his eyes but that voice made me crazy. It was a stomping in socked feet on a kitchen floor, that voice. It reminded me of all the mothering he needed.

I told him goodnight, that I'd be right up. But it was my birthday and I wasn't tired at all. I went to the kitchen, to the bottles of good wine Staffy kept on the bottom rung of the cheap wooden wine rack. Already knew which one I wanted. The bottle had a plain white label and fancy silver writing. I held it in my hand, felt the weight of it. The bottle said, ...*valley in the south of France.* It said, *earthy* and *chocolate* and *berries.* It said, *According to the Surgeon General....*

I imagined Staffy's sense of hearing was heightened since his pupils were so sore. Removing the cork, I was very careful. I suffocated the sound with a green plaid dish towel. The smell of the good, aged wine was stronger than I was ready for. It launched a gulp of nausea high into my throat. But I waited it out. I stood in the kitchen and breathed my breath until the nausea passed into a familiar dull chunk inside my chest.

The lights were off and the living room window was

open to the early fall air and I sat on the built-in window seat with my bottle of wine. No sense wasting a glass. When the baby was born I'd be up nights a lot. I imagined a blanketed lump in my arms. I put my wine bottle down and held my arms out, imagining the tiny weight, cradling the invisible air. I don't know. It just felt like holding nothing. It seemed possible that it could be born and I might not love it. It seemed possible that it could be born and I would never feel a thing.

Through the open window, there was the sound of a car driving by out front. I could tell from the rattle of the engine that it was German, and I could tell that it didn't come to a full and complete stop at the stop sign. Assholes.

One big birthday sip, a toast to me. I thought, if I was a tree I'd have thirty-one rings. Then I heard the insistent rattle of the German engine again, this time it slowed down a lot coming past, and then drew to a stop on the street side of our hedges.

This was it.

I almost dropped the bottle of wine, almost fell up the stairs I was running so fast to tell Staffy, this was what he'd been waiting for. But he was asleep already, open-mouthed and breathy. I put my ear up to the open bedroom window and heard the engine by the hedges still running. Hurry. Wait, what if the grass is damp? Maybe I should bring a blanket. My god, it's not a picnic, woman. Move. Get out there. Go. I said that last *go* out loud, too loud, and Staffy's breathing stopped. He turned onto his side, and when he did, I took one nice big sip from the bottle and I knew that I didn't want him to come with me anyway. I wanted to do this alone. It was my fucking birthday.

I headed out to the backyard.

. . .

This is me: Delilah Seward. Five months pregnant. Hand around the neck of the bottle of good wine. Wexby Industrial Super Search Eye Spotlight. Crouched on my haunches behind the big green hedges, crouched down low. Except, being pregnant, I couldn't crouch that well. I listened.

The German rattling stopped, and the car tick-ticked as it cooled. Even though the hedges were as wide as a sidewalk, they were just leaves and branches and air after all, and sound traveled through them like nothing was in sound's way. I could hear the faraway freeway and the underneath noise of 82nd Avenue. I could hear the persistent late night birdcalls and wondered which birds are the birds that are up so late.

The German car's windows must have been rolled down because I heard Led Zeppelin singing from the other side of the hedge, and then I heard it click off. My breath stuck at my throat, and a jolt of panic went off in me: that strong loud quiet, all of us strangers, all so close. It made my heart race. And the race traveled up to my brain and back down to my heart past my stomach and then it landed in my gut. My bowels to be exact. Perfect.

Sound of the car's old springs as bodies moved around inside.

The man's voice was close. "Let's go," he said.

A woman's voice, an accent, Russian maybe.

He said, "You said fifty." His voice sounded mean, the way mean sounds when it's scared. "I gave you fifty."

She said, "Shhh."

He said, "Hurry. Oh. Good. Yes."

And it seemed so obvious right then: it's the men, not the women. It's the men.

My stomach and intestines started making noises, angry gurgling, impossible to ignore. That fucking pot pie.

From the hedges, the man's voice again. "Good," he said. "Good, yeah."

It was intimate and sickening, and made my stomachache worse. I suddenly missed being a kid, before sidewalks and marriage and overgrown hedges. I missed being small. How Staffy must feel all the time. Like he just wants to be taken care of.

The hedges said, "Oh, God."

The hedges said something like, "The other one too."

I don't know what I thought I'd hear. I don't know what the hell I was doing. All I could feel was my nervous gut. I really needed to fart.

The hedges said something like, "This one?"

I looked up and there were the stars, dim pins of light in the sky. My Super Search Eye was slung over my shoulder, thanks to its handy nylon carrying belt. My Super Search Eye like a star of my own.

Another sip. Just a small sip. I could almost smell the sex through the hedges. As far as I could tell, it was just normal stuff. Just lumps of flesh bumping into each other. No wonder people have to pay for it.

The man raised his voice then. One sharp, quick cry.

Air stayed in my lungs and wouldn't budge. Me listening, all of us quiet. That cry made me want to throw my head into the hedges, just to be near something else alive.

Air sneaked out of my lungs. The sounds of everything began to fade back in.

Then the whine of a car door in need of oil, opening. The woman's voice, her accent. "No," she said, "Here is fine." And the metal chunk of the door slamming shut.

The turn of the engine, German rattling, the engine driving away, and then the sound of high heels walking on asphalt, the sound of walking away.

Just me now, by the hedges. Alone, the way I like it. Still had plenty of good wine left in the bottle, still half full.

Heard another car drive by, stop at the stop sign, and keep going. It all started doing laps in my head. The wine and the sexy stuff and the listening. All of it. I felt gross. Everything was gross. I needed to lie down, so I did. Me and my belly, we lowered ourselves onto the grass by the overgrown hedges. Splayed out like an angel, the damp against my arms.

It was late, early late, and the stars were really going now. Dulled a little by the city's light, but still, I could see them. The stars shone and winked. But nothing shot. Up there, just dust and rocks and light and darkness.

Next Monday was my 20-week appointment with the ultrasound technician, the one where we see the baby, learn the sex, where they check all its organs and brain and important parts and make sure everything's okay. I was scared to go.

The great big sky was over me, the moon already gone. I thought of all the nights I'd soon be up shushing that baby to sleep. I thought of diapers and burp cloths and the way new baby houses smelled like sour regurgitated milk.

And then I thought of the cake, my cake, waiting on the countertop. And the candle. That one perfect candle, all mine, waiting to be wished.

SAVING THE ANIMALS

My boss Barb is wearing her tailored black raincoat with her pajamas underneath. Her short gray hair blows in the wind, almost straight up. She cups her hands around her mouth to send her voice out as far as possible, past the walking path and toward the Bay. Almost midnight, it's impossible to see anything or anyone out in the black water.

"Goo-ooose," she calls.

That's what she's named him. Goose.

Barb looks back at me under the streetlight, leaning against my folks' car, my arms hugging my body to keep warm. Her voice calls down.

"Christ, Mindy. Do something. Help me yell." She turns back toward the dark water and calls his name again. The wind eats her voice.

I scramble up the embankment, over the vegetation, my feet unsteady on the slippery leaves and hard roots, and then I am onto the bike path in the freezing dark.

I've been working for Barb since getting out of college, sixteen years. I know her so well I don't need her to tell me what she's thinking — her voice is already going in my head, what she wants, when she needs it, who she wants me to call. Even so, I never saw this thing with Goose coming.

My social life exasperates Barb. To my face she encourages me, says, "get out there," as if *there* is a specific place I need to go where at last I'll find myself surrounded by all the men I can't otherwise manage to meet. But away from my face I've heard her say other more direct things. I've overheard her talking to her son on the phone more than once. *Depressed,* she says. *Dependent,* she says. *Desperate to be married.* She says, *Well, she could be attractive if she'd color her hair, lose a few pounds, and wear some blush.* She says, *No, I certainly don't want you asking her out.*

At the very least, Barb wants me to spend time out of the house, with anybody other than my parents. Yes, well I am out now. I am spending time with Barb in the middle of the night at the foot of a bridge looking for a goose. This is an excellent example of why I prefer to stay home.

Home for me is the attic apartment of my parent's house. We call it the attic but really it's a weird addition they threw on top of the house when I was in high school — just a project so my dad and my brother Louis could spend time together. They built it themselves without a permit and didn't consult a single professional. The roof leaks when it rains and the floor is so thin my folks and I talk to each other right through it. What else I don't like is that the only entrance is through the main house, through the living room, past the kitchen and up the bare wood stairs. All in all, though, it's a pretty good deal. They only charge four hundred a month. Most nights I can hear them underneath me, my family, like an ocean, they make so much goddamn noise. TV is the only way to drown them out.

I am an embarrassment to my father because all the rest of my cousins are now married. I mean the women. In my family, nobody cares if the men marry or not. The men are allowed to stay home indefinitely, mooch off the parents and live like slobs. But the women. I'm talking about the women. The only other single cousin, Mara, was just married last month. She stood up at the altar next to a dog of a man and said okay instead of I do. When the floor cleared for their first dance she took her time getting up there, slugged a shot of Jameson with me, strapped her shoes back on and walked into the hazy spotlight. Just like that, she's a wife.

Me, Barb says I'm not putting myself out there. I try to listen to Barb because she's my boss and even though she yells a lot I respect her. She's really made something of herself, head of her own design company, and she goes out of her way to support me. But I also don't listen too hard because Barb's not married either, not anymore. Also, she's a little loony, for example bringing me out here in the middle of the night to call a goose back home. Home being the business park pond where the goose used to live. Before Barb drove him down here this afternoon to the foot of the bridge to save him.

Times like these I wish more than one person worked for Barb. Once a month and at tax time the accountant comes and sits at one of the empty desks in back by the copier. Otherwise it is me and her and nobody else.

It wasn't just that Goose got used to Barb walking down to the pond at lunch to feed him popcorn. No, Goose was part of the problem too. If Barb missed a day, Goose would scuttle up the grassy hill and over to Barb's big office window that looks out on the business park pond and trees. He'd peck his bill right on the glass in single syllable greetings. Hi. You. Hey.

Barb would shriek like it was George Clooney outside. "Mindy! Goose is back."

It's true that the window was a large wall of glass at ground level, but even so, I didn't understand how a goose could see through any window. They have these little round eyes, and each eye is facing out on the opposite side of their head. But there he was, watching Barb, his feathered head tracking her, moving whenever she moved.

It said a lot about me that Barb could get a goose and I couldn't even get a man.

I don't think Barb planned what happened today. It was just a normal Tuesday at first. Coffee, client emails, Barb barking for one file or another. As always, she'd been out first thing that morning to toss popcorn to the geese, and when lunchtime came Goose walked up the shallow grass slope to tap at her window. My desk was just outside her door, and because I didn't have a window and there was nothing to see, listening was what I got good at.

My face was in the MacKenzie file.

The wheels of Barb's leather office chair squawked. "Shit," Barb said. "Here comes Raul."

Raul was the building security guard and he was not a fan of the geese, and definitely not of Goose, and particularly not of the Barb/Goose relationship.

I heard the familiar dull knocking of goose bill against glass. Then Barb's voice. "Shoo," she said. "Get."

I pretended to keep my mind on Mr. MacKenzie's file.

Now it sounded like Barb's knuckles were rapping the glass. Barb's voice. "Don't you touch him!" She charged past me out of her office and the stack of correspondence in the MacKenzie file fluttered.

"That jackass," she said.

I pretended to keep working until she was out the front door, then I hustled into her office to watch through the big picture window.

There was Raul, shaped like a yam with arms and legs. His tiny eyes and clenched lips overtaken like an avalanche by his big mound of a head. His face mostly stubbly flesh with features designed for a much smaller man. Barb's muted mouth opened and closed, her eyes scrunched into tiny slivers, crow's feet erupting from their corners. Her nude stockings and black high heels right up against his black security boots, feet wide apart. The tips of her fingers poked into his doughboy chest. He smiled his tight little security guard smile through Barb's assault, but I could see his worry underneath — Barb's love for that goose was unpredictable in its ferocity. His eyes jumped to find mine through the window and I shook my head. No way, my eyes said back. I ain't helping you, buddy.

I knew Raul. We went to high school together and he was mean then too. One time junior year he asked me if I'd like to go to the winter formal with him and when I said I would he said I bet you would but I wouldn't want to go with you. That was a long time ago, I know, but still, I'm okay with watching as he's publicly humiliated, spanked by the wrath of Barb's voice.

By the time Barb returns, I'm back at my desk creating a new client folder. Her cheeks are flushed from yelling.

Barb says, "Now he's saying it's not him. It's the cleaning crew."

The phone rings and I answer. "Good morning. Barbara Trevor Design."

Barb keeps talking. "He says the cleaning crew says it's because of his shit up here by the window. They don't like cleaning up all that shit."

"That would be me I guess," I say to the phone.

Barb says, "Then Raul threatened him. Said don't get

too attached. Said sometimes these geese, they just disappear."

I say, "We are very happy with our current copy machine. Thank you." I hang up.

"Can I go to lunch now?" I say.

Every day I eat my lunch at the pond, a cheese and bologna sandwich and corn chips, unless it's raining or too cold. There are three benches by the pond and one is the one in the shade where the geese don't poop much. That's where I sit. Even though I know the pond is a fake put here by the business park architects, I still find it peaceful. There are little birch trees and green grass and a fountain spitting up in the middle of the water.

The geese usually come visit at my bench while I eat but I do not feed them and they do not bother me and I play a game where I try to guess which one is Goose.

The sandwich was down the hatch and I was snacking on chips when Barb out of nowhere stood next to me in her tailored black raincoat, carrying a dirty green towel. Her purse was over her shoulder.

"Are you going home for lunch?" I said.

Barb said, "I'm going to pull my car around front. I want you to grab him from behind."

Initially I thought she was talking about Raul. I don't think I could get my arms around Raul if I tried.

She said, "He'll come over when he sees this." Out of her giant mouth of a purse she pulled a bag of popcorn. Her other arm held out the dirty towel. "And you'll need this."

I did not reach for the towel. Barb tossed it next to me on the bench. Technically, I was still at lunch.

Barb shook the bag of popcorn like a pom-pom and

started calling across the pond. "Hi Goose. Here comes my Goose. What a good goose you are. What a good goose. Do you want to go for a ride in my car? Yes you do. Yes you do."

Sure enough, the gaggle tramped toward us, their geese breasts stuck out proud. I stood up from the bench. My corn chips fell off my lap and the animals swarmed and pecked at the pile.

"This one. See the difference?" Barb said. "He has a particular intelligence." She pointed at one as his neck extended and he pecked the ground.

Barb said, "I'll be one second." She handed me the bag of popcorn and hurried toward her car in the lot behind me.

My pulse began beating loud in my ears and I understood it to be saying, *You do not want to steal a goose.*

There he was at my feet. Pecking bill. The dirty towel under my arm.

Familiar pit in my gut that said no when I did not. My quiet voice croaked out a call.

"Good Goose," I said. My hand tossed him a puffy kernel. "Good boy." I didn't know how to talk to a goose.

Barb's engine turned over in the parking lot, and Goose looked toward the noise like maybe he did want to go. She threw the passenger door open from inside and leaned her body over the armrest.

She yelled from the car. "Grab him from behind and stick him right here." Her hand patted the seat.

"Oh hell," I said to myself. I do not normally swear. Not ever. Across the pond, the UPS guy Gary hopped out of his truck in his little brown shorts and waved to me on his way into the building. I waved back. Normal, normal, my wave said. Everything normal.

My eyes met Goose's eyes. I took a long look at him.

His long black legs and pretty feathers that from far away look black and brown but up close are actually lots of colors which remind me of sand and copper and coal.

I held the towel open like wings and whispered *Sorry* and lunged for Goose, grabbing him from behind.

His wings had sharp elbows. I hugged him to my chest like a squiggly baby.

He clucked and honked, his wings tried to flap, bits of his feathers floated up and stuck to my lips.

Ahead of me stretched the grassy expanse that led to Barb's BMW parked sideways in the handicapped spot, passenger door flung open. The distance elongated with each step I took. I had no idea how many seconds it would take to get there. It might take forever. It occurred to me pond geese might be protected by some kind of law. It occurred to me I could go to jail, and then seemed certain. I'm going to go to jail. I'll be in jail for kidnapping a big feathery bird and no man will ever marry me. I will never be a bride. I'll die an old maid like Aunt Louisa, hiding Snickers wrappers in my couch cushion and eating dinner at four in the afternoon.

"Looking good," Barb said.

That's when I felt it on my wrist, warm and wet. He'd pooped on me, which, when I thought about it, seemed like an appropriate response to being kidnapped.

I knelt into the open door of the passenger side and plopped Goose in.

Barb said, "You poor thing. You're covered in poop." She was talking to the goose. She held him down while I shut his door and climbed into the backseat.

Once he was in the car Goose was weirdly calm.

He sat in the front seat sideways just like I'd left him, the dirty towel with feathers and poop around his feet. He was facing Barb, turning his head left and then right, left and then right.

"See," Barb said. "I told you."

I wasn't sure if she was talking to me or the goose.

"He knows we're trying to help him," she said. "He wants our help."

I stayed quiet in back.

Every time I'm in Barb's BMW I'm amazed by the interior. Black leather seats and a fancy navigation system with maps and buttons and lights that remind me of a plane's cockpit. If I had a fancy car I'd never put a goose in it, but Barb is funny like that. Borrowing her car to drive ten blocks to pick up sandwiches for a client meeting is out of the question, but she'll let a pooped-up goose ride shotgun.

Barb flipped a U-turn and drove out of the lot.

Goose let out a loud honk.

"I know," Barb said.

He tried to fly at the windshield.

"I'm sorry," she said. "My poor baby."

Out my side window the office park pond looked normal, the water feature spitting water into the air, the trees hanging over the sides of the pond. The stone benches empty. Everything like it was supposed to be. Just one goose short.

The car was going slow through the streets of Foster City. We passed the big mall and the diner whose waffles I like. The radio was on, chatter about the stock market. The tick tick of Barb's blinker as she moved over a lane.

Goose aimed his long neck at the roof of the car. Let loose a low moo that climbed to a proper honk.

"Hold tight," Barb said. "We're almost there."

The BMW turned off Hillsdale Boulevard onto a small side street and entered one of the subdivisions built on top of the marsh. All of Foster City is built on marshland. Originally the marsh stretched from San Mateo to the Bay, an intermediary between land and water. Then in the sixties developers came through and put cement over the marshland and built a bunch of lookalike houses and people moved in. Finally they slapped a bike path onto the perimeter of everything. It traces the edge of the man-made land so the people can jog and pedal and push strollers while looking out across all that water.

Barb picked a street and headed east/southeast according to her cockpit controls. We drove through the neighborhood. There were not a lot of trees. A woman my age in sweatpants stood next to an open minivan door yelling at someone inside. Farther down a knocked-over pink tricycle rested on its side in a broad cement driveway. A big white boat asleep under a blue tarp.

The street spit us out against the embankment below the bike path not too far from the foot of the long white San Mateo Bridge.

Barb parked her car against the sidewalk next to an incline of green vegetation. I could make out the bridge's rush of moving traffic, the sound in competition with the water on the other side of the incline lapping against the rocks.

The three of us sat in the quiet car.

I watched a seagull through the car window. It caught a rise of wind over the Bay.

"I don't see any other geese," I said.

"That's ridiculous. Of course there are geese here. Geese love water. Why do you think they're always around that pond?" Barb said. "It's because of the water."

When Barb got out of the car I did too. She walked around to the passenger door and opened it wide. Goose erupted from the car in an awkward takeoff, one wing catching on the car frame. He hobbled to the embankment's incline of vegetation that separates the street from the bike path. Ruffled himself, shook his tail feathers, spread his wings as far as they'd open, and honked out one big cry.

Goose walked up the incline and we followed him. Barb in her black suit and black high heels. Me in my slacks and flats. My sweat staining the underarms of my work blouse.

The water lapped against the rocks. The traffic off a ways on the bridge. A bicyclist sped by me. A lady in red shorts was jogging farther down the path.

"I don't see any other geese," I said again.

Goose pecked his bill at the ground.

"Will you be okay here?" Barb said. "Do you think you can make some new friends?"

Goose spread his wings and flapped them around and laid them back against his chest.

"Well, all right then," Barb said. "Goodbye to you too."

On the return trip it was very quiet. I sat in the back again. Radio on low, some kind of news. The car was like a crime scene, Goose's bunched up towel on the passenger seat, grassy wild poop smell. When Barb pulled into the office lot and parked, neither of us got out.

Big white clouds floated low in the blue sky. I could see them reflected in the windows of the office building.

"That was right, wasn't it?" she said. "What we did?"

A light wind tugged at the branches of the trees surrounding the pond.

"I guess," I said. "I don't know."

"Oh Jesus, Mindy. Have a fucking opinion sometimes." Barb blew her nose. Sniffed. I couldn't tell if she was crying or if her allergies were acting up.

I got out of the car and walked past the pond, the bench, the trees. The rest of the geese were on the other side of the grass now, pecking. Two were swimming together in the pond.

For the rest of the day we didn't say much. Even the phone barely rang. I typed client letters on the computer and ate an old bag of peanut M&Ms I found at the back of my desk drawer. At the end of the day I called goodnight to Barb without poking my head in the door and I did not look over when I walked past the pond.

Deep into my nighttime ritual, I'm reading in bed, hand in an open bag of Milano cookies, my cat Roger asleep on his side at my feet. The phone rings. I share a landline with my parents downstairs, but I don't answer it because it's never for me.

My mom shouts through the floor.

"It's Barb," she says.

I pull jeans on over my pajamas. Grab my purse and my dad's old heavy wool flannel shirt that I wear like a jacket and head downstairs. I can hear a TV talking behind my parents' bedroom door.

I put my head close to the shut door and listen, just to have a moment to myself.

I knock twice. I say, "It's me."

My dad says, "Duh."

I poke my head through the open door. I cannot see

their faces, just two sets of feet sticking up under bed covers facing the nightly news.

I say, "I need to borrow the car. Is that okay?"

My dad says, "You'll never get a man to marry you with a boss like that. You might as well marry her instead."

My mom says, "My keys are on the entry table."

Roger follows me down the stairs, his metal tag clanging with each step. Louis is where he always is, in the living room, feet in socks, stretched out on Dad's brown corduroy recliner. Football on the TV.

"There's a game on right now?" I ask.

"Don't be an idiot" Louis says. "It's a rerun of the NFC Championship game from '82. Cowboys and the Niners. Fucking classic."

Green field. Different colored outfits running from one side of the screen to the other. The colors washed out like it was a photograph left in the sun. "Do you know how it ends?" I say.

"Of course I know," Louis says. "Why would I want to watch an old game I don't know how it ends?"

The furnace kicks on. Air pushed through the vents. I grab Mom's keys from the entry table.

"You got a booty call?" Louis says.

"Very funny," I say. "I have to meet Barb."

"Mom and dad think you're a lesbian, you know."

"Shut up, Louis," I say. "That's just dad."

"I'm just saying," he says.

It's chilly and, despite the dark, I can see fog rolling in over the hills. My big flannel should be warm enough but the damn wind is blowing and my ears are cold. Barb is walking along the path calling for Goose. She is visible and then not under the tall street lamps' umbrellas of light. Visible, then not. Visible, then not.

I head the opposite direction on the path, north along the water.

I can hear the sound of water against rock just past the path and a muffled angry truck horn from far off and everything in the Bay is black except for the lights on the bridge trailing the seven miles to the other side of the Bay where there is finally land again. Lights overhead blink red and white reflected in the water from the sky as a plane heads for SFO to land and empty out its passengers.

I'm alone except for Barb way behind me, everything dark except for the umbrellas of light. It feels good to be out here in nowhere by myself late at night.

Headed away from her, there is no way for me to hear Barb's voice. It doesn't matter. We will never find the goose. I know this. But for Barb's sake I try.

"Goose," I say. It's more of an insistent whisper.

"Goose. Goose. Goose."

The long white snaking bones of the bridge stretched over the black water. The blowing wind and quiet sky.

"Goose," I say. I am louder now.

What do I know. Maybe he's out there. Maybe I'm wrong.

"Goose!" I say again.

"Goose!" I use my whole voice.

And there. I see something. Is that him? That could be a goose, out a ways in the water, sailing the chop on top of the Bay. I stop and listen. The sound of easy nighttime traffic, the Bay's rhythmic touching to shore, the tall fingers of dry grass rustling together in the wind.

I stop calling his name.

Yes, that's enough. It's enough to think maybe.

I'M YOUR MAN

The hospital is much farther away than we imagined, two freeways, across town, over a hill, and of course the doctor's office is in the farthest possible building from the garage where we park our Honda snugged up with the hundreds of other cars shiny wet from the cold rain.

Already, we are fifteen minutes late for Bert's appointment.

We run through the parking garage, Bert first, loping like one leg is shorter than the other. Me second, purse bobbing on my shoulder, hand holding a large jar full of coffee because it's the goddamn crack of dawn.

We are through the sliding glass doors, up the elevator, down the hall.

The receptionist sees us coming. She stumbles over the name. She says, "Bert Hanny-fan?"

Close enough. She waves us past.

She says, "Go on in. Ask for Sarah." She says, "Just pay after."

We run-walk down the corridor. Loping Bert, bobbing purse.

We swarm the first woman in scrubs we see. One of us says, "Sarah?"

Sarah says, "Come with me."

Sarah takes us past the nurse's station, computers, phones. Fluorescent lights. Blue carpeting. It smells like chemicals and warm Xerox paper. A couple of other faces in scrubs stare out at us. They must all know how late we are. We are late. So late. We are awful. This is what they are thinking.

Sarah says, "Get on the scale."

Bert hands me his winter coat.

Sarah says, "Two fifteen."

Bert says, "Two fifteen?"

I don't know where he hides all that weight. I look for it. There is some extra on his belly.

Sarah says, "Step against the wall."

She looks at the wall. She says, "Seventy two, a little more."

She writes on a piece of paper in a file folder.

Sarah walks fast down the hall. We are expected to follow. Her blue scrubs look suddenly comfortable, like work pajamas. I could use some work pajamas.

I am holding Bert's heavy winter coat, wearing mine, purse bobbing. In my free hand is the large jar filled with coffee and cream and that warmth against my palm is keeping me steady.

Sarah stands to the side of an open door. She says, "You're right in here."

We sit in the small room. It is already crowded. Bert is on the papered exam table and I'm on a loveseat smooshed into the corner. The loveseat is pink pleather cushions and wooden arms and legs, something out of a medical office catalogue under the heading: Make Your Patients Feel Right At Home.

I am still holding everything, coats, purse, coffee jar. I heave the pile over onto the cushion next to me, unscrew the jar and, praise god, I hit the coffee, three quick chugs.

On the wall is a poster that shows the inside of a penis, capillaries and vessels in sharp reds and blues. Next to that in the corner is the mandatory metal sink with tall-necked faucet like the top of an f, stinky-clean medical hand soap, automatic paper towel dispenser, and above all that on the cabinet door a sign says, *We're all in this together.*

Bert says, "I'm nervous."

I say, "There's nothing to be nervous about."

He says, "What if the doctor wants to cut my penis open?"

"That's crazy," I say. "You sound crazy. It's an office visit."

This is when the door opens and a woman with a long horsey face walks in. Straight dark blonde hair, low cut black sweater, short black skirt, black stockings, and black knee-high boots. Obligatory white coat.

She says, "I am Dr. Foote."

Her voice like the edge of a serrated knife.

She will not look us in the eyes for more than a small part of a second. When she speaks to us she speaks to her clipboard.

She says, "We don't have much time."

"I'm sorry," I say. "We had no idea how far away it was."

Her lips spread a bit. A smile, maybe.

"This will be a short appointment," she says. "I have other patients."

She lowers herself onto a round black stool. The wheels squeak as she settles in.

Without moving our bodies, Bert and I look at each other. Look back at Dr. Foote.

The three of us make a triangle, Dr. Foote on her stool, me on the loveseat, Bert with legs dangling from the papered exam table.

I take another hit of coffee. I drink too fast and it gets

caught in my throat. When I am done coughing, Dr. Foote speaks to her clipboard.

"How long have you been trying?"

Bert and I look at the doctor not looking at us. Our voices hopscotch.

Me: "One year." Bert: "About a year."

Dr. Foote writes on the clipboard.

She says, "Your hormone tests came back with a slight elevation of prolactin. Doesn't mean anything. All appears normal."

Sound of a page turned in the file. Paper creased by a hand. Scratching of pen onto paper to test the ink. She is in love with that clipboard.

To Bert up high on his table, she begins her barrage of questions. "Do you smoke?"

"No."

"Drinking, how much per week?"

Bert says, "Per week? Maybe seven drinks?" His eyes meet mine. "Ten?" Sure, ten sounds good. No need to mention Bert drinks like a dock worker.

Dr. Foote crosses her legs revealing her black-stockinged knee above her boot. "Any street drugs?"

Bert says, "No."

Dr. Foote's eyes swing to me. My stomach flip flops.

"Not even marijuana?" She's talking to Bert but looking at me, like I am his pusher, like I've got a nickel bag and a pipe in my purse and we're just waiting until she leaves the room to toke up.

Bert swallows. "No," he says. "Not anymore."

"And you don't wear tight pants on a regular basis? Bike shorts, what have you?"

The squeak and click of the stool's metal wheels against hospital floor. She pushes a little bit forward, a little bit back to find the right spot before she continues.

The jar of coffee in my hand suddenly seems ridiculous. I'm not relaxing at a café on the Seine. I chug the rest, replace the lid, set it down on the floor.

Dr. Foote says, "The results of your semen analysis show a slightly lower count than normal."

Bert says, "Right." We've heard this before.

She says, "Not a huge deal."

She says, "Your motility is a bit low, and percentage of normal sperm is quite low."

Bert says, "Right. Wait, what?"

This we have not heard before. What does she mean? How's a normal sperm supposed to act? I picture Bert's wayward little guys painting their fingernails black, getting tattoos.

She swivels to the loveseat. Again her eyes land on me. "And you? Ovulating? Healthy? Everything functioning normally?"

But already her long horsey face is back in her clipboard.

"We thought it was me," I say. I clear my throat. "My eggs, you know, because often it's the woman. I took that test where they inject this..."

She swivels back to Bert. "Well, let's do a quick exam."

Rising from her stool, the doctor sets her precious clipboard on the counter by the sink. "Stand up and drop your pants and underwear to the floor."

Bert's expression says, *Yikes!*

I point at me and then point at the door, like, you want me to leave? Bert shakes his head no.

From a cardboard box Dr. Foote pulls a pair of heavy blue latex gloves, stretches them over her hands.

Bert stands, unfastens his belt, his pants and boxers fall to the floor. The doctor's blue hands reach out.

I turn my head toward the pile on the loveseat, cross

my legs, pick up my purse. I look really hard for something to look for. My hand trolls the bottom of the bag.
Keys; pen; chapstick! Perfect. Put on that chapstick, take
your time. Really smooth that waxy chapstick all over
your lips.

Dr. Foote's blue hands feel Bert's testicles.

Do not stare. This is all perfectly normal.

The sounds of give and stretch of blue latex over skin.

I check my purse again. Probably I should put on some
more chapstick. Yup, that's better. Maybe I'll just check
my phone. No messages. All-righty. No problem. There's
probably an old mint in here somewhere.

Dr. Foote says, "Okay."

Oh thank god.

Bert leans down to pull up his pants.

The doctor says, "Now just turn around and lean
against the exam table. I'll check the prostate."

Bert's expression says, *Mommy, no!*

Or maybe it says, let's just not do this. We don't need a
baby. We could travel the world or own a bed & breakfast.

Bert in profile: pants around his legs, elbows on the
table. He turns his head to look at me, wide round eyes.
What can I do?

A little toothpaste tube of lubricant, her blue finger like
the toothbrush.

The room shrinks. Bert and me and Dr. Foote, we are
too close, if I stretch I could touch Bert's elbow, touch the
hem of her white lab coat with the tip of my shoe. No matter how I try, I cannot turn off my ears.

I aim my eyes at the metal sink and focus focus focus
until Bert and the doctor are just smudged shapes in my
peripheral vision.

I try to take a breath. The pleather of the loveseat
squeegees underneath me.

Dr. Foote says, "Try and relax."

An excruciating silence. I'd kill for some lite jazz right about now.

Dr. Foote says, "Ready?"

I am really concentrating on the sink and the counter, and *We're all in this together.* The sounds inside the quiet kick in, HVAC air moving in the building, a door clicking shut down the hall.

Bert says, "Ah. Ah. Oof." He breathes out.

The doctor says, "Sorry, but I have to get up there."

The coffee is a scum-topped pond in the basin of my belly.

The doctor says, "Just relax. Now let's try again."

Unnameable silence. Stretching of latex.

Bert's ruptured breathing. A sharp intake of air. He lets out a hard laugh. His laugh says embarrassment, pain.

I sink into the loveseat. I make myself small. My body is a rope in a knot pulled tight.

A woman in the hall laughs.

The exam table paper scrunches under Bert's elbows.

I want to disappear. If I stare at the wall long enough I will disappear. I will become the wall.

Bert says, "Ow. Ow. Ow."

I am not here.

Bert says, "Aaaaaggh."

I shrink into the couch. I close my eyes. I drop my face into my hands, open palms hot against my cheeks.

"Sorry," the doctor says. "Okay."

Snap of latex as the blue gloves come off. Warm inside body smell in the air.

When I open my eyes Bert is leaning forward, elbows still on the table, pants still at his ankles.

Dr. Foote walks to the trash, tosses the blue gloves. Her knee-high boot heels click clack on the floor.

I want to throw up. I think I might need to throw up.

The doctor says, "You may get dressed."

Bert bends over and pulls up his pants, his belt buckle rattling. The air in the room feels soiled. I start to uncurl my body, but I cannot seem to unclench my jaw.

Bert and I, we do not look at each other. We must not look at each other. Instead, I look at the coffee jar on the floor. It was present during the exam and is obviously now a biohazard and must be destroyed.

Dr. Foote says, "Well, your testicles are quite small. Smaller than normal. Have you always had small testicles?"

Bert says, "I don't think so. I mean I think they're the same as always."

I think about Bert's testicles.

I say, "I've never noticed a difference in size. Over time. Not compared to other testicles."

I stop talking. She must hate us. She clearly hates us.

Dr. Foote sits down again on the little stool. The wheels squeak. She is writing fast in the file. She is writing about Bert's testicles. She is writing that they are small.

Bert sits on the exam table. I'm still frozen on the loveseat. We've got to get out of here.

To her clipboard the doctor says, "Let's order another semen analysis and look at the results and talk more then."

She stands up. Precious clipboard cradled against her chest.

Her right hand irons the front of her white coat. "Well," she says. "I'm leaving."

"Should we stay here?" I say.

"No, I mean I'm leaving the country," she says. "So for a while there's not much I can do."

Bert says, "Where are you going?"

"Africa," she says. "For a month."

I picture her immunizing crying babies and caring for the elderly. Maybe we got off on the wrong foot. Perhaps I've misjudged her. We *were* fifteen minutes late after all.

She says, "On safari."

I reconsider.

Her body is straight as a line. She says, "I'll send Sarah in with a cup for another sample."

She pivots away from us on the heel of one of her black knee-high boots. She leaves the door wide open.

Bert says, "Have a good time in Africa."

Yes, un-bon voyage.

The quiet room. Somewhere down the hall is the muffled sound of a toilet flushing.

"I hope she gets eaten by a tiger," I say.

Bert says, "There are no tigers in Africa."

"Fine," I say. "I hope she gets eaten by a lion."

Sarah, the nurse, walks in.

"No, not you," I say.

We're back at reception. Bert carries a paper bag with his sample cup inside, the bag's top carefully folded over like a school lunch.

The receptionist says, "Mr. Hanny-fan?"

Bert says, "Close enough."

She says, "So that's one fifty for today's visit."

Bert's hand sets his school lunch on the counter, pulls the checkbook from his inside coat pocket, and starts writing out the check.

The receptionist clacks on her keyboard. At her elbow the phone rings, but she does not answer. I look out the big picture window at the parking garage.

The receptionist says to Bert, "Here's your copy."

. . .

Back at the elevators. Bert's finger on the down arrow.

My heavy winter coat on. Somehow I am now carrying the school lunch.

The down arrow button lit up. We wait.

The ding before the doors open.

"I'm going to say it out loud," I say.

"Don't do that," Bert says.

The doors open. Me first, then Bert. The doors close. Our bodies tucked safe inside the pocket of the elevator.

Down we go.

Instead I say, "I hate winter."

Bert grabs my free hand. School lunch in the other.

The elevator swings the tiniest bit from side to side, the quiet knocking in the mechanics of it all, the cables and wheels and pulleys, everything holding us in mid-air.

The ding before the doors open on the ground floor.

The doors open.

There's a couple waiting to get on. The man carries an empty infant carseat. In the lady's arms is a tiny baby, eyes closed, pug nose, mouth open. A baby so tiny it is mostly blanket.

We do not move from the elevator's pocket. We do not make room for them.

The lady with her blanket baby steps forward to squish on with us.

"Sorry," Bert says. "No." He waves them off the elevator. "You'll need to take the next one. Wrong floor." Bert starts fake coughing. "And I have a terrible cold." Cough, cough.

He never lets go of my hand.

The couple back away with their tiny baby to wait on the other side of the open doors again.

Bert's finger presses the up button.

Again.

Again.

My hand in Bert's hand. My other, the school lunch.

The baby starts to squirm in its blanket.

Any second now the doors will close. We can start again. Back to the motion of the rocking elevator, everything working together, the cables and wheels and pulleys, and Bert and me safe in mid-air.

SURE FOOTING

Love lasts until the man you love leaves because he wants to drive a truck up and down the I-5, hauling for a Central Valley feed company in the blazing hot sun and endless brown miles.

He tells you over dinner.

You are bringing a forkful of chicken and rice to your open lips.

He says, "You won't need to leave the porch light on anymore."

You do not have another fight in you. You're sick of thinking up reasons for him to stay.

You say, "Sounds like a good idea. You love to drive."

And in that moment he's gone. The distance is growing like he's already started driving away.

You think it's for the best because after he's been gone for a handful of days you admit to yourself that maybe what he was wasn't love.

It's early morning, still no sun. It's quiet and dark and you're sitting in your favorite orange chair, looking out the window, drinking strong black coffee that smells so good you don't want to ruin it by taking a sip, but eventually you do anyway, and damn, if that's not just how a cup of coffee should taste.

The feel of that hot sip moves over your tongue, down your throat to your empty stomach, warming all your insides on its way. That sip is further proof you shouldn't be together because when he makes coffee it's watery and dull and waking up to it is not the same.

There is a hint of orange blue sunrise near the tops of the pine trees and you open the window a crack even though it's twenty degrees and there's white frost covering the grass and cars.

The fresh smell of cold and morning and pine slaps your face.

A couple seasons. Your hair is longer. You don't miss him. You've been alone long enough now to get used to your own sounds and no one else's.

It's a Friday. You're listening to music, Carl Smith on the record player, and you're chopping onions for supper. You get a five minute warning call from the gas station across town before he comes by the apartment to visit. You hear gears downshifting, a release of air and the hard metal clank of chains as the eighteen-wheeler comes to a stop outside.

You peek through the window.

On the side of the truck is a picture of a grazing cow and the words *Hornby Feed* branded on its flank. When you open the front door you can smell it coming off him, the slaughterhouses, manure, dust and heat.

"Mind if she sits out here for a bit."

He's gained weight. His tee-shirt is tight across his middle and his blue jeans are soiled, stains and creases cover his lap. He's starting to grow a beard or hasn't shaved. You can't tell which.

"I'm on my route," he says. "Headed back. Took a shot you might be home."

He talks different too, you think. It's unfamiliar and odd.

It's kind of a turn on. Makes you wonder who he's having sex with these days. Hookers. Other truckers. You know the deal: you've seen *Cops*.

His hands fumble at his sides, then he pushes them into his front pockets, then moves them to the back, like the awkward appendages are brand new. He calms them down by reaching forward and touching your hair, the split ends that you've grown since he left. His touch is clumsy and unwanted but his fingers smell like Borax and his nails are clean. He must have washed up at the gas station, you think. That single kindness is a crowbar swing at the clamped shut heart you've come to love keeping to yourself.

He says, "Wouldn't it be funny if we'd been married all this time. If I was just coming home after driving all day."

His words remind you of everything you hated about him: you are not a prize at the end of the day. You are not in line to be anyone's wife. They also remind you of having him around, the sounds of the weight of him on the floorboards and the stairs, the fresh damp smell of his just having shaved, the quiet of his slow breathing when you first wake up.

He's going to ruin everything.

He stinks like wet tobacco and diesel, but when he asks without asking you take him up to bed. It's sloppy and quick and afterwards he falls asleep with his mouth wide open.

Next morning he's up before you.

"It's the shift," he says. "I'm usually down past Modesto by now."

He stands in the kitchen wearing a pair of your old sweatpants, faded pink, that stretch taut against the shirtless bulk of his belly.

And then you smell it. It's hidden underneath layers of lemon-scented floor wax and wet rice from dinner two nights ago and garbage that needs to go out to the curb, but it's there: the smell of fresh coffee.

"Sometimes when I'm driving, I let myself remember how you look, like this, in the morning," he says. "When your hair is uncombed and tied back, your bare neck right there."

Even though he's not touching you, you feel his fingers on your skin.

"You like to drive," you say. "You love to drive."

The cold floor against your bare feet is sending shivers up into your shoulder blades. You're sure that's what it is, the cold floor.

Through the kitchen doorway you can see through the living room window past the front porch onto the street where his truck rests outside. You cannot remember if he broke your heart.

He goes to the cabinet. You wish he wouldn't. You know what's coming.

"I'm so tired," you say. You mean lonely. You mean weak.

He hands you a coffee cup, brings the warm pot over because you can't seem to move yourself. He pours the hot coffee into the pink ceramic mug, your favorite, he knows. It smells mighty good. The hot of the coffee heats the mug and warms your fingers that wrap around it. You cannot remember if you broke his heart. You cannot remember if you were glad he left. You lean your head down. You go in for the sip.

GOOD COMPANY

1.

We are heading toward Vegas, driving toward night, the windshield cracked and dusty. Sand on the side of the road looks like snow through the headlights and for a second I get excited because Christmas isn't Christmas without the snow. Ahead is a stretch of thin clouds pulling purple and orange to either side. There are red taillights in front of us, lights coming toward us and moving away, lights in the rearview. All of us in motion. I am driving because I am always driving because Marcus does not drive. His license expired a long time ago, back when I still had bangs. I am not wearing my glasses like I know I should and never do because they make me look old and ugly. Without them even the white reflective letters on green highway signs can be difficult to read unless I squint and concentrate.

Henderson, Nevada used to be nowhere, ten miles before downtown. And now it is a place people say they are from. We are on our way to see his parents and we are not getting along and I hate him.

We are having the argument we always have.

"It was fine in college," I say, "but now it's ridiculous."

He says, "But I didn't wear shorts in college. I'm just getting into this look now."

"They aren't even really shorts," I say. "Just cut off pants." My God, I am my mother.

He says, "You sound like your mother."

"And when you do wear pants," I say, "you wear flip-flops with them and then your naked feet just stare at me even though your legs are finally covered up."

He says nothing, directs his stare that could halt a herd of buffalo at the windshield. His freckled hands rest on his freckled knees which are right there because of course he is wearing shorts.

To the windshield he says, "I packed my good jeans."

To the windshield he says, "Look out," because I am looking at him in disgust and ahead of me are bright red brake lights braking.

Off the exit, over a two-lane road carving a way between sand and brush and mountains on the right and sand and brush and Las Vegas on the left, past a little all-night market with neon exclaiming *Liquor!* My hair is twisted in tiny knots from the long miles of open windows, which always makes me feel wild and pretty and free until I see my reflection. We take a left and pull into Red Meadow Desert Community and pass a guardhouse that is guard-less, just for show. Any yahoo welcome to come right in. We drive through the wide clean treeless streets.

I have never met his parents before but this is what I know: The Dad is mean and smart, self-taught on books and the History Channel. He's small and orderly, "…and you'd better be polite." The Mother is taller, a redhead, allergic to everything. Her meals consist mostly of fruits and vegetables and only certain grains juiced together in a blender, "… and you'd better not make fun." Sometimes she eats bacon though. And sometimes she smokes cigarettes.

I pull to the curb. Marcus says, "Also, she is sort of

dying." I park. He says, "She's been dying for years."

Her dying makes me want her to like me.

"Eventually. We don't really know when," he says. "I think she uses this to her advantage." He laughs a dry, raspy laugh and says, "That sounds horrible." He stops laughing.

The house looks like all the other houses, desert pink and dark and quiet.

He says, "I've got to take a shit."

His slammed door rocks the car side to side. The far mountains are black silhouettes and Marcus, from the sidewalk, says, "Come on."

The front yard is a garden of rocks and nothing else. He jogs up the clean, broad cement driveway and I follow dragging my vintage Samsonite, made before the invention of luggage with wheels but purchased after at a thrift store. Our arrival triggers the floodlights. The ground below me still feels like road under tires at seventy miles per hour, the speeding and rocking.

The Dad stands waiting in the open front door and shakes hands with his son, then me, perhaps the kind of people that do not hug. The History Channel really is on in the background and it smells like air freshener, clean and unfamiliar.

Marcus jogs in and waves. He pushes short loud breaths through rounded lips, like a woman about to give birth.

He says, "Can I use your bathroom?" Passing by the half guest bath off the entrance he says, "I don't want anyone to hear."

The Dad emits a gruff snort and shuts the front door. A piece of small notebook paper, torn from its spiral binding, is taped over the inside of the front door's peep-hole.

The Dad sees me looking at it and says, "So people can't look in from outside."

The Mother is out of sight but I hear her say, "Are you filled up on junk? I can make dinner."

I carry my Samsonite into the foyer and there is the Mother in a suit and nylons and fluffy blue slippers. She is motioning with a section of the newspaper to a juicer. I act like I cannot feel her eyes on my knotted hair, my jeans worn through the knees. Too old, she must be thinking, to be dressing like this.

I wave and say, "Hi," too loud. It is quieter after.

I smile. Here is a woman who does not need me to like her. She holds up a finger and says, "Just a moment." She walks back into the kitchen, her slippers scuffing against floor.

I say, "It's nice to meet you," not looking at anyone in particular.

The Dad and I stand in haphazard formation, like strangers in an elevator. A black cat sits in the foyer with us then walks to the couch, claws the arms. The Mother says, "Brooklyn!" The cat stops clawing and stares at me, patient.

Against a wall, tucked into an oak media cabinet, the television flickers black and white images of helmeted troops marching by, leaders hovering around a map on a table, a cluster of bombers flying low to the ground, and under it all a low grumble of indecipherable narration. I concentrate on seeming like someone who is perfectly comfortable. Standing here. Not saying anything.

The living and dining rooms and kitchen are all one open area. The Dad sweeps a quick hand around, furniture, walls, vertical blinds, and says, "Caroline, they call it the Great Room." Then he looks back at the television screen. A large ficus in the corner displays Christmas cards. On the coffee table is a manger the size of a shoe-box, Mary, Joseph and the baby Jesus in a huddle. I think to say they have a nice home. I do not say it. When Marcus emerges from his parents' bathroom he brings the smell of soap back with him and heads wordless to the kitchen to open cabinets and look for snacks. The cat wanders to the coffee table, stands on her back legs and grabs the tiny Mary with pointy teeth, bats it around with paws under the table. The Mother says, "Brooklyn!" And she drops it.

The guestroom is all bed and no room and this is where I will be staying because we are not married and Marcus was raised Catholic. The door doesn't shut — mid-swing it bumps into the bed. The lack of privacy is familiar, an uncomfortable reminder of my own mom's insistence on open doors in our house at all times.

On the wall hangs a gold-framed landscape of pastel mountain shadows, a pastel river. Behind parted ruffle curtains, outside the window my view is the massive central air unit that keeps the house the perfect tempera-ture all year round. I drop my Samsonite and do not unpack. I hate unpacking. It's depressing and messy and a daily reminder that I will have to pack everything back up again in a few days just to go home. With nothing else to do, I leave my suitcase on the bed and walk into the Great Room, the television on, volume loud. The TV says, "Circle gets the square," to a couch of the Dad and Marcus. They do not look up. I am invisible. I head for the Mother.

She is in the kitchen sitting on a wooden stool, right leg crossed over left. From a radio next to her, though it's hard to hear over the roar of Hollywood Squares, I catch what sounds like maybe a fiddle and guitar underneath a man's voice. Head down, reading glasses pushed to the bridge of her nose, she concentrates on the *New York Times* crossword puzzle. I recognize it right away. The Saturday puzzle.

"Mrs. Walters?" I say. Bathrobe, nylons, slippers.

"Don't call me Mrs. Walters and I won't call you Ms. Kendall. We are not co-workers." And without looking up says, "Call me Marianne."

I say, "I smoke. I need a lighter. Sorry to bother you."

The Mother puts the pencil down, pushes the reading glasses onto her head and says, "I'll come with you."

Out the sliding glass doors on the patio are two plastic Adirondack chairs, a palm tree the size of a person growing in a glazed pot, and a pair of worn flip-flops. The yellow porch light is on. The Mother retrieves an ashtray from behind the palm tree and sets it on her bathrobed knee. She lights her cigarette first, takes a drag, then hands me the lighter. The ashtray says *Hawaii* in big rainbow letters.

The desert night is cool and thick and quiet. But I can hear the rush of the faraway freeway and the constant whir of a planned community of air conditioners.

"Hear that?" she says and exhales smoke. "When you live here you get used to the forced air. Hot or cold, it doesn't matter. If I go to turn it off I feel like I'm going to suffocate." Then she uses her cigarette to point up. There are stars up there, lots of them, visible despite the light from the Strip, its invasive megawatt neon. I see Orion without even trying.

I inhale the luscious, rough nicotine. "Marianne was my mom's sister's name," I say. Smoke out through my nose. "But she died a long time ago, before I was born." The word *died* sits with us awhile. "So it feels funny to call her my aunt."

My feet are bare on the cool cement. I cover one naked foot with the other.

"Sorry about that door," she says. "I told him that bed was too damn big in there."

I'm smoking Parliament Lights because they're not too expensive and I like the blue across the white pack. The mother has Nat Shermans. Through the glass door I see Marcus, the dad. Two heads facing a television.

"I try and smoke only once a week since I started juicing, since the diagnosis really," she says. "But it's Christmas."

Fingers pick at invisible lint on her robe. Her red hair is swept up in a compact bun, dyed now probably, bobby pins controlling any strays, flawless. She stares at the nearby lights of a neighbor's house as I stare at her. It doesn't occur to me to look away.

She says, "I am not going to spend the last years of my life counting cigarettes." She points her lit, brown-papered Nat Sherman at me and says, "I like you."

I try not to smile. I say, "Thank you," because I don't know what else to say. Instead I exhale and aim the smoke up to the rocky chunk of waning moon.

"We celebrate a more traditional Christmas," the Mother says. "I'm sure Marcus told you? We're Catholic, but Walt hates all the hoo-haa, the shopping and the commercialism. Especially Santa. He thinks Santa Claus is weird."

"Oh," I say. "Yeah, he is kind of."

"Usually I push harder to incorporate some of the normal stuff, the stockings at least, a tree. But this year, I don't know. I wanted to let him have the whole strange thing the way he wants it."

I am going through another phase where I recognize

how disgusting smoking is, but still I finish the cigarette. I smoke it down to the filter.

"I imagine it will be more like a birthday party for Jesus," she says. "You'll be sleeping in the guest room. And Marcus will be in the den."

I nod my head and try to seem respectful. "I know."

The Mother holds out the ashtray and I stub my Parliament Light into the bottom where it says *Hawaii.*

"I like you," she says again. I smile.

The men turn their heads, waving hands in front of their noses as we come in from smoking outside, and then we all sit around the coffee table, divide up the brass bowl of nuts, and play poker next to the shoebox manger. Whole nuts still in their shells. Peanuts a nickel. Almonds a quarter. And walnuts with their carved, indented channels the big kahuna at a dollar. I do not help my situation much when I eat two dollars and fifty five cents worth of assets. We play until I am left with only papery red peanut sleeves and the Dad has everything and Marcus pretends to fall asleep at the table. He is a sore loser.

The Mother checks her hands. She says, "I'm going to pay for that." She scratches her neck, red marks there now. "Peanuts make me swell."

She goes back to her stool in the kitchen and begins to swallow her vitamins, prescriptions, herbs and oils, lined up next to the stove like spices. I flash on what that row of supplements will look like when the Mother is dead, how they will likely sit there for months, nobody willing to move them, nobody wanting anything else to change.

Morning. Breakfast is flax and berries and green powder

and juice and yogurt mashed up in a blender. Afterwards Marcus and I say we're heading out to the store, but really we'll drive around in search of a place to have sex. We tell his parents we need a special battery for my camera, that my folks will want to see pictures of the weekend, and when the Dad pulls open his battery drawer in the cool dark of the garage, pointing to the various shapes in their lettered packaging, I am happy to stand with him, lean over the drawer and say, "No, not that one. No, not that one. No, not that one."

Marcus and I are going on two years together but we have sex like couples that have been married for twenty. Not in terms of frequency — we do it a lot. But we do it the way a person might do something really challenging over and over again with no real hope of reward, like taking the SATs for the tenth time to raise a score above 1,000. A labor of love, without the love part.

We drive down the road to the market exclaiming *Liquor!* and buy condoms. I'm at the register when a tow truck pulls into the lot and the driver steps inside. He grabs the men's room key and says, "Reggie, can I borrow a newspaper?"

Reggie is sixty maybe, tattoos on each forearm. "He'll be in there for a while. Second time today." He rings me up with a wink. "Every morning," Reggie says. "Wish I was that regular."

I walk fast out the door and tell Marcus to park on the far side of the lot next to the tow truck.

I say, " Let's do it here."

"What?"

"You big baby. We have tinted windows," I say.

The sex we used to have, it was miraculous — several times a day, every day. But with the months passing and the relationship outside of sex not what it used to be, I suspect us of maintaining the frequency as proof that everything's fine. After all, the sex is usually the first thing to go, but here we are, we can tell ourselves, doing it just as much as we did a year ago. Sometimes we tell our friends to make them jealous. Sometimes it works.

I re-park the boxy Nissan, one spot between us and the tow truck. Our windows have that tinted sticky film on them, poor man's privacy, so I am not that worried.

We push the front seats forward and have sex in the parking lot in the backseat on top of damp sunflower seed shells and a dilapidated copy of *Adbusters* magazine I do not recognize as ours. I am on my back and Marcus is on top of me, trying to finish. This could go on for a while and the broad daylight cannot be helping. I pull the magazine out from underneath me and look closer, see stamped on its cover "Waiting Room Copy Dr. Robert Adele, Chiropractor" and remember now why I took it, the article about the dangers of fluoride, how the country of Belgium has banned it entirely and how I would like to finish that article so I can discuss the subject with anyone and not sound like I don't know what I am talking about. His eyes squeezed shut, Marcus is trying. He is trying.

I take a breath to say, *It…*

He says, "Shut up."

I wait. And then nothing.

He says, "Sorry." Our usual stopping point.

I have tried to stop saying, *it doesn't matter*. It's not only him. The last time I came with Marcus was over the summer during the heat wave. He forgets about this, I think.

He says, "It's broad daylight. And this fucking car, I can't fit in here on top of you and concentrate. It's impossible." He punches the driver's seat headrest.

I prop up on my elbows, slither out from under him

and grab my jacket, not to put it on but to fish a cigarette
from the inside pocket. Marcus hates that I smoke, but I
hate that we can't come. While I smoke, I think, *God, I love
smoking*, and flip through Dr. Adele's magazine. Marcus
pulls off the condom and throws it on the car floor. I could
script out what transpires next.

Marcus says, "Why do we even bother using these?"
He turns away and finishes himself off. His breath slows,
he zips up.

He does his best to recline across the backseat, his bare
legs and freckles over my thighs, catches his breath. He
does not look at me, just stares up at the inside canopy of
the Nissan, the thousands of pin size holes, and says, "I
don't even know what we're doing here. My parents are
freaks. They don't do a normal Christmas. Not anymore."

I hear feet walking on gravel. The tow truck door
slams shut. The monstrous engine starts up.

Marcus says, "You could go right now. Maybe you
should go. You can take the car."

The sun is taking over, high above the roofline of the
Liquor! store. I push my skirt back down and sit up, lower
the backseat window. I consider leaving, everything that
means. A car pulls up two spaces over and parks, a whisp-
ery trumpet and Billie Holiday's voice escaping from the
open passenger window. The driver leaves the engine
running, hops out, change jangling in a pocket as he hur-
ries into the store.

"You want me to go?" I say.

Marcus makes like he doesn't hear me and gets out of
the car. He smoothes his shorts down, says, "Do I look
okay?"

Without waiting for an answer he says, "Be right back."

Billie is singing two spots over, a bluesy piano underneath her voice now. I stare into that car, someone else's

life right there, the ignition still on. I tell myself not to think. I tell myself thinking gets in the way. So I leave everything in the Nissan and walk over to the Billie Holiday passenger door and unlock it through the open window. I tell myself, do not look around. I get in. I sit in the running car. Everything is fine. I think to myself, should I take my purse? I turn and look toward the *Liquor!* store entrance. No one's coming. I jump back out, walk to the Nissan, grab my purse from the floor behind the driver's seat next to the useless condom. I take Dr. Adele's magazine too. I wait for what happens next.

I hear him before I see him, the quarters in his pocket. He does not get in.

He pokes his head through the open driver's window. "What the fuck?"

If my life was a beer commercial he would be hot in a grubby sort of way, and I would be hot in an obvious sort of way and probably wearing a half-shirt that reached just past my erect nipples, dangerous high heels, my hair wild, unkempt. He'd hand me a six-pack, the cold bottles steaming in the desert air. I'd hoist it all in my lap and rub his buff, dirty biceps as we drive off, not wearing seatbelts, tires kicking dust into the parking lot behind us.

Instead he is grubby and gross, sweaty, overweight, and high on something that makes his eyes seem separate from his head. He is already drinking what he bought inside, can of Schlitz popped open. My nipples are not erect. It dawns on me, this is a terrible mistake and I need to get out of this car. And at the same time he says, "Get the fuck out of my car."

To the empty parking lot he says, "Somebody get this crazy bitch out of my car."

Marcus comes out of the *Liquor!* store, ignores the ranting man. I do not take a moment to consider whether

I should try and smooth things over.

"Sorry," I say. My purse on my shoulder. "Wrong car," I say. I open the door. "Sorry. Sorry." Idiotic smile.

He gets in his car and he and Billie drive away. "Fucking crazy bitches," coming from the driver side. I don't understand how I could have it so wrong, how someone like that could like Billie Holiday.

Marcus hands me a new pack of Parliament Lights and the minty gum I like to chew right after I smoke. He leans on our car. Bare legs under his shorts. Stares at the sun, at the now quiet parking lot of the *Liquor!* store. I see that Marcus is hot in a grubby sort of way. And he doesn't not like Billie Holiday. Also I realize I left Dr. Adele's magazine in that other car. I will never know about Belgium, about fluoride. There is not a lot to say. This is not the first time I have done something crazy and then stopped before the crazy thing actually started.

Back down the two-lane highway, through the guardless gate, empty lookalike streets. Relentless sun. Marcus stops at the front door, stands on the welcome mat. He looks at the closed door ahead of him. He does not look at me. The back of his head, his bare neck, my favorite part of him.

He says, "No. Don't go. I don't know why I said that."

He hands me a cardboard backed small, single battery. He says, "For the camera."

2.

The Dad is wearing black slacks, shined black leather shoes, a white pressed shirt. We watch him fold up a black polyester vest and slip it into a slim fake leather briefcase. He offers us a ride into town in the hushed, soft interior of the white Cadillac from the late 1980s that sits on the left side of the garage. This is the Dad's car. The Mother has her own — blue, sensible, foreign. He tells us it might be nice to be in his car, a nice car, for a change. Nothing against the car you drove here. That car's just fine.

From the cool dark of the garage to the warm late afternoon winter light of the desert. He moves the gearshift, R to D.

The Dad is driving in to start his shift as one of the banker attendants stationed in the middle of the open overwhelming chaos of the casino floor at Caesar's Palace.

He says to Marcus. "Not a job they give to just any-body." Loose skin crests over the clean tight collar of his work shirt as he turns his head.

He talks to us through Marcus. If he has a question for me, he will look at Marcus and ask the question with my name slapped onto the end of the sentence.

To Marcus, he says, "Have you been to Las Vegas before, Caroline?" Marcus twists in his seat, looks back at me.

I say, "I've been to Reno."

And the Dad turns back to the road and says, "It is not the same."

Quiet for the rest of the drive.

Three heavy slams of American metal doors.

We park the Cadillac on the roof of the Caesar's Palace parking garage. The Dad says, "By the last light pole on the north side. Don't forget."

The sun is closer to the horizon but the sky is still bright. The Dad carries the slim briefcase under his arm, close to his body. I sat next to it on the drive to town and I could see everything. Important things inside. Folded work vest. A paperback Webster's Collegiate dictionary

missing most of the front cover. A wrist watch I have yet
to see him wear on his wrist. When he opens the briefcase
to check the time a strong odor of aftershave wafts out
from the inside. It is not unpleasant.

He looks at the watch and says, "I'm early. I'd like to
know if you want to eat breakfast with me."

He looks at Marcus and says, "Marcus knows this," and
then explains that before his late afternoon shift he likes
to eat a good breakfast to help his body adjust to the
unusual hours.

He says, "I have discovered my favorite breakfast buffet
is in the Caesar's Palace. But they don't serve as late as the
Bellagio does on Sundays. Remember that for next time."

We follow him as he walks down the parking garage's
cement stairs. Nobody says anything. We follow the Dad
until we are standing together, the three of us on the
sidewalk. We wait to cross at the light on the Strip.

The Dad is mostly bald. I am several inches taller than
him even in my sneakers and I can see the thin gray wisps
straggling from one side of his head to the other. Trim.
Compact. He does not take up much space. I imagine that
as a child he looked exactly the same, briefcase and all. But
he is a presence despite his size. And there is some kind of
sadness there underneath his fastidiousness, something
rarely pointed to. A mouth of a memory swims to the
surface. I cannot see the whole thing. But there is something, Marcus telling me his Dad was an orphan, adopted
late in childhood. Is that right? It sinks again. Disappears.
I do not see the Dad in Marcus at all. Which frightens me.
Because if it hasn't come out yet, I am sure it will.

"Also, they have champagne," he says. "I do not like
champagne but I know Marcus does."

The Dad looks at Marcus. "Do you like champagne,
Caroline?"

On the corner are newspaper stands of red, yellow, green, stocked with newspapers made up of advertisements for prostitutes. In the pictures the lighting is bad and all the prostitutes are displaying their gargantuan breasts and as much of everything else as possible. Free porn, everywhere. Shoe-scuffed. Tire-marked. On the sidewalk. In the street. Blowing past when the wind picks up.

"I do," I say. "I love champagne."

We cross and head for the Bellagio. I step on one of the prostitute's tattered breasts in the crosswalk.

The Dad says, "The Bellagio serves breakfast via the buffet until 4:00 p.m."

Marcus says, "You already said that, Dad."

And the Dad says, "No. I did not. I simply said the Bellagio serves breakfast later."

There is a couple with matching Iron Maiden tee-shirts walking ahead of us. Maybe they know about the buffet too.

The Dad stops on the sidewalk and hands Marcus the keys to the quiet Cadillac and says, "Please just bring the car back to me before I am off at midnight. Thank you."

My legs are cold. I should have worn pants.

He looks at Marcus and says, "I think you'll see it drives much better than your car, Caroline. I think you'll like it."

It dawns on me what a big deal this is, how he must never let anybody borrow the Cadillac ever. And I do suddenly see the Dad in Marcus. The relunctant kindness. The type of man a person grows into loving. And how after the Mother is gone the Dad will be alone. No one else willing to put in the time. It pushes up into my throat, and I do not know if I can eat anything at all.

"And if I did like champagne, still, I don't drink before

work," he says.

Marcus puts the keys in his pocket and grabs my hand for the first time in a long time. His hand is warm and fits into mine perfectly and I feel lucky that I have anybody's hand to hold at all. The automatic doors open and wind rushes down from the desert mountains through the long, straight Strip and follows us as we enter the Bellagio. My hair is lifted up, covers my eyes, lands its sharp tips.

The Dad says, "You know who loves champagne?"

He points us towards the buffet and says, "It's my treat."

The food is not good but the booths are nice, brass and leather. Before Marcus goes back up for a second helping the Dad sips his sweating water glass, dips his linen napkin in his glass, wipes his mouth and says, "I'm off."

We walk through the landscape of green felt and loud patterned carpeting. The deep pocket of the Craps table with its boxes and numbers and brazen COME across the basin, the smoky half globes of cameras on the ceiling, perfume, cologne, women's bare shoulders, men in tracksuits.

Marcus says, "Don't they pump oxygen into these places?"

We pass the synthesized singing of a group of slot machines, like squat levered birds. Plastic chips fall into other plastic chips, deadened against the quiet of felt. Clapping at one of the tables next to us. As we pass the clicking spin of a roulette wheel, the dealer says, "No more bets."

We walk by a cluster of nickel slots, a car mounted on top, what a player might win, flashing yellow lights to get someone's attention. They get Marcus's attention.

He points to one of the machines. "This one."

He sits down on the stool and says, "Go get me some nickels."

He says, "Sorry. Be right back." And goes to get his own damn nickels.

I know enough to sit on the stool in front of the one he wants to play. So I sit. Three machines over, a woman sits on her motorized cart, a Li'l Rascal, pulls the long lever. She looks into the columns of bright fruit and dollar signs that whirl by. She pushes nickels in, does not see me looking at her, does not see me looking at the place where the hem of her pants fails to meet the top of her sock, her skin exposed, pale, almost blue. Mounted on her steering handles is a miniature American flag and a picture of a teenage boy in a blue dress shirt, collar up, dark eyes, no smile. She wants that car.

A cocktail waitress comes by, all legs and shoulders and space between her breasts and says, "You're supposed to be playing." She looks around her. She says, "But if you want to order something, honey, that's fine by me. What you want?"

When she brings the two beers back, Marcus says, "Thanks." He tips her two dollars and he does not look at her breasts. I love this about him.

I say, "We should have ordered champagne." But Marcus is already playing.

I stand over his shoulder and watch. He plays a second and a third round. He plays long enough for the symbols to line up in a sequence that sounds an arpeggio of digital notes and makes the yellow light mounted on his machine whirl and whirl, nickel after nickel dropping into the plastic bucket he holds underneath the machine's open mouth.

Marcus has a look on his face like he deserves this, like he knew.

I wonder what the cut-off point is, when the dollar amount is too high, too many nickels to let them fall out of the machine. One hundred nickels? A thousand? The L'il Rascal neighbor looks over, watches the stream of coins drop into the bucket.

"Asshole," she says. "At least you didn't win the car."

I also hate him a little bit right now. And I don't know why. He'll share his nickels with me. It's not that. It's the noise of the casino, and the noise of the machines, and the lights, and all these people. My heart beats loud and fast, too fast. Black splotches spot my vision, bigger and bigger, and there is not enough air. I need air. I need a cigarette. I need sex, but real sex with someone who can come while still inside me. And right before I go black I think, I don't even know what day it is.

I am never certain what happens between knowing it's coming and knowing it's over, but I can hear Marcus saying, *she does this all the time.* He's saying, *she is fine, see?* I am on my side on the floor, the weight of my body on his body. Slumped against him, coming to, for a moment I feel safe and he seems strong and I think before I can stop myself, *Marcus knows how to take care of me.*

A man, middle-aged, overweight, his hair unnaturally black, he is the first thing I see.

He says to Marcus, "I came right over." There are bits of fat and hair visible in the small open spaces between his hardworking buttons and I think he might be looking up my skirt.

He takes a drink from his beer bottle and says, "I'm

very observant." And after a few seconds he wanders away.

I am not quite ready to move yet, but Marcus says, "Ready?" and I say okay and he helps me to my feet. He's wearing my purse over his shoulder, casual, confident, as if it is his purse.

He sits me at our machine. "Are you okay? I fucking hate when you do that."

His eyes are big, wild, and they scan around the casino, like he is scared, like I matter.

"Got to cash in these nickels. Can I leave you here?"

I don't want him to leave me here. But he does. And I say nothing.

He walks away to cash in his plastic bucket of nickels. Sitting at our machine, the world going on around me, everything still spinning, I feel exposed, a rock in the middle of a river.

The waitress with the legs and the breasts comes over and says, "Sorry, you're gonna have to leave."

But she says she can get me some water first. "Do you want some water?"

"I'm waiting for my boyfriend. I'm okay," I say.

She smiles the way she might smile to a lost dog in a park, and I wish suddenly I were her friend. I wish we'd come here together, me and her, to this stupid casino. I'm not here with Marcus and she's not here with her bare shoulders and drink tray. She laughs at my passing out, at my ridiculousness, lets me lean on her shoulder until we're outside. We stumble back to our shared hotel room and consume an overpriced minibar Snickers and a bottle of rum. We watch bad TV and she reenacts my fainting again and again and I laugh until I can't take it anymore, until I double over onto the floor and beg her to stop.

She says, "You okay?"

The faraway corners of the room will not sit still.

"I'm not drunk," I say. "I'm a fainter. I faint."

But she has turned away, walking toward another customer, and perhaps I am a little drunk too.

In the Dad's quiet Cadillac, we are one car in a row of cars on the roof of the Caesar's Palace parking garage. Up here the city surrounds us. Cold and obscene and rough at street level, but a few floors up, after fainting, it shines. The flame of gold lights — it's like looking at another galaxy, a chaos now ordered and tranquil. Through the windshield the sky is a dark underwater blue, the faraway outline of the mountains darker, almost black, impossibly far.

Marcus says, "Every time it happens I hope it never happens again."

His jaw tight, he tells me it's like I die for a minute — my eyes rolled back and my mouth open and my tongue hanging a little bit out.

He grinds his teeth and looks away from the peaceful burn of the flat city, gazing out the driver side window onto the heavy Roman arches of Caesar's Palace. He says, "It's not pretty."

Back in LA, all this is easier. I wake up each morning and look out our second story window right onto nearby rooftops, into the open windows of surrounding apartment buildings, a block of parked cars, a mattress left on a strip of dry grass. There is the roar of traffic on Hollywood Blvd, the raised breakfast voices of Armenian neighbors, mockingbirds mocking the trill of a car alarm. I drag a match to light my morning cigarette and in the smog cannot see much past the palm fronds two blocks up. In LA, Marcus's shorts make sense and when I smoke that first perfect cigarette of the day, before talking, before coffee, it is easy to believe that we are thriving and strong and alive.

Dull click of heels on asphalt as a woman crosses the parking lot. She passes illuminated from lamp post to lamp post, tosses her hair from side to side, stops to look inside her purse, continues on.

"Let's go back," I say.

To Henderson. To LA. To before.

His jaw still tight. "Yeah," he says. Gaze still aimed out the window, at the outside world. For the first time it occurs to me that Marcus might want out too.

"Good call," he says.

We sit in traffic on the freeway toward Henderson even though we will have to come right back in a couple hours to pick up the Dad, to do this all over again.

Marcus turns the radio dial, listens for what he wants. Static, chatter, the abrasive mellow of light jazz.

I pull the visor down and there I am in the little illuminated makeup mirror.

"Look at all these cars," Marcus says. He lands on classic rock, keeps searching.

In the little mirror my face appears giant and flawed, one feature at a time.

"A thousand idiots sitting in their fucking cars," he says. Low chorus of strings, quiet in the way quiet only is right before it gets loud.

"Leave it here," I say. But he doesn't.

"And my dad in that shitty vest taking people's money or their credit or whatever." Dial to Air Supply. He says, "I hate this song."

One eye, my lips, my imperfect teeth. I flip the visor up.

"You just won thirty-five dollars," I say.

He settles on Frank Sinatra.

He smiles to the windshield and says, "Yeah, that was pretty cool."

Off the exit ramp, down the two-lane highway past the *Liquor!* store, through the guardless gate and around the blocks of clay-colored houses, some bright with fat colored bulbs outlining their architecture, others just standing dark and silent like nobody's home, like today isn't Christmas Eve at all. Marcus rolls the Cadillac into the garage. The Mother's sensible foreign car gone.

The house is quiet and I am tired so I shut the guest-room door as far as it will shut, the space that remains still wide enough for a person to fit through. I move my suit-case and lie down on the bed and when I close my eyes I am bobbing around in a lonely little boat pushing away from the shore. I open my eyes and realize that I am still drunk and have not yet eaten dinner and before much longer I need to decide if I am going to be the me who sobers up and remembers to act like an adult, or the me who decides not to care, who foregoes dinner and what others might think and keeps on drinking until the long list of things I am supposed to remember fades to a dull smudge. This is the most un-Christmasy Christmas ever.

Marcus stands in the doorway, in the person-size space, and I don't need to be a genius to know what he is think-ing. As much as he hates my fainting, he loves it too. It does something to him and afterwards he can always come, no problem. So without permission, in his parent's house on Christmas Eve with Brooklyn the cat watching from the open doorway, we have sex.

I take off most of my clothes but leave my shirt, my bra, the things I know he likes to play with. He pushes his shorts and boxers down until his feet can take over and get them off all the way. He is already inside me. He hovers above my body, eyes closed, and I make the sounds he likes. I can smell the shampoo he uses, a cheap brand always on the bottom shelf at the store, a shampoo that is really a shampoo and conditioner in one.

My arms are splayed out like I am on the cross. I do not touch his back or shoulders or ass. I cannot do it all. But I know what he is waiting for so I concentrate and let go and Marcus can tell because his Oh Gods turn into Oh Carolines and just like that, he comes. He keeps pumping his body against mine, trying to get out every last bit, like he doesn't want it to end, like he knows he doesn't know how long until the next time.

The room is dark and we are lit by the streetlight through the window on one side and the light in the hallway on the other. He rolls off me and even though it is dim I know he is smiling. He throws his feet in the air, tube socks still on, and lets out a shout.

"Fuck yeah!" He slaps my bare ass. "You should pass out more often."

But as soon as he says it we both know he is sorry. Because it does not seem so funny that I pass out, that he can come right after.

Already it is cold here on top of the bedspread, Marcus beside me. I listen for the sensible foreign car's hum or the rough rumble of the garage door. I look for red brake lights reflected on the ceiling. But there is nothing.

The quiet and the dark open up around me and finally again I can think. Tomorrow is Christmas and I do not have presents for anybody, not even Marcus. The Mother said no hoo-haa, but would it be an insult to buy them gifts? Should I get something for Jesus instead? It is his birthday. What do you buy for Jesus that your boyfriend's parents might also use for themselves? Especially the

Mother. Something good for Jesus and the Mother.

My tee-shirt is wrenched up above my breasts, bunched around my neck where Marcus left it. This is all I am wearing. I have never felt at ease being naked around Marcus. With other men this was never a problem, but with Marcus I am always one step behind myself. Uncomfortable and naked, I'm waiting for the Mother to come home and find us like this.

"What kind of cancer does your mom have?" I say.

He says, "They don't like to talk about it."

He says, "And I never said it was cancer."

In the dark Marcus is difficult to see. He says, "Relax, will you?"

He is careless in his nudity, finally proud of the freckled body he was born with. He's told me that growing up was torture, his freckles like the plague. In gym class he never showered with the other kids.

I take a breath and close my eyes and focus on letting go a little bit of the everything that I'm holding onto: gifts, Marcus and me, the Mother dying of whatever it is she's dying of.

As if he can read my mind, Marcus rolls over and pulls me toward him. His body shapes itself around mine.

"No. Wait," he says. "You spoon me."

He flips over first and I follow. I do my best to fit all of me around all of him, but he is taller and my lips rest against the back of his neck. This is as far as I can reach. We settle our bodies together, snug like the continents before they drifted apart. Maybe tonight I do not need to eat dinner after all.

Marcus breathes his deep sleep breathing. I cover him with the half of the bedspread he is not sleeping on. I find my skirt and underwear and bra on the floor, and when I walk out to the Great Room and turn on the lights I see that I've put my skirt on inside-out and backwards, the hems showing, tags in front. I push the skirt around my hips till the tags are in back but as for the inside-out I just don't care. Brooklyn sits on the top of the couch facing the dark television screen. I have the distinct impression that she knows what we did and does not approve. In the kitchen cabinets I cannot find what I'm looking for. There is a box of cereal, a can of beans, the Mother's tidy row of supplements and vitamins and herbs next to the stove.

In the middle of the kitchen, on the bottom shelf of the island behind some club soda and sparkling water, is a tall bottle of tequila, sauza, the good stuff. I reach and weave the heavy bottle through the foreground of mixers. The bottles clank, the sound ringing around the room. I am a loud inconsiderate drunk. In the sink is a glass, previously used, dirty finger smudges at the base and more smudges from someone's lips at the rim. But the size is perfect and when I sniff inside the glass it smells like nothing, probably water, so it will do. I'm getting a little excited now and I need a cigarette obviously, and the anticipation makes me think I need to pee but when I unscrew the cap of the bottle and the sharp, dirty bloat of the smell of good tequila hits me hard, I know that all I need is this. The sting sits at the back of my throat, a wallop of warmth and heat, and just then I hear what I have been waiting for, the heavy grumble of the garage door. The clock on the microwave says seven-fifteen. I do not have a plan. I do not run back to wake Marcus up, to tell him to get dressed. I do not put the tequila away. I can feel Marcus's semen running out of me, down my leg. It is not something that happens very often and I remember that we did not use a condom, which we never forget to do since I refuse to go on the pill: I am not one of those women who will do anything just to make it easier for a man. And the kitchen door opens and the Mother walks in.

She is carrying two paper grocery bags with the name of a store I do not recognize across the side, and a plastic bag with party supplies peeking out the top, the shiny letters of a banner, paper plates.

I ask if I can help but she is already inside the kitchen, two feet from the counter by the stove, and after taking one of the grocery bags I just set it on the counter that she was about to set it on anyway.

The Mother is no fool and I see her eyes go to the open bottle of sauza, the good stuff, on the island, my skirt on inside-out. I feel dirty and I know I smell like her son and I know what she is about to ask and because I do not want to be facing her when I tell her the truth, I turn away to wash my hands in the warm water of the island sink.

She sets her purse on the counter and says, "Where's Marcus?"

I do not lie. "He's asleep."

The Mother says, "Well, I can use your help."

In the garage it is dark, the overhead light has timed out and the Mother and I stand at the open trunk of her sensible blue foreign car, next to the Dad's Cadillac that Marcus and I will need to drive back to pick up the Dad at midnight. With the Mother I stare into the shallow well, lit by the little yellow trunk light. Lying there flat against the carpeted floor is a long cakebox of white paperboard.

The Mother says, "You take this side."

We navigate the garage, past the battery drawer I scoured with the Dad, and I balance my half of the cake on my knee while I open the kitchen door and then we deliver the big flat box to the counter next to the open bottle of tequila.

The Mother leans her hip against the countertop. "I am exhausted."

Her perfect red hair falls down in accidental sprays from her bun. On her forehead is a thin layer of sweat, the wisps stuck there, and under her eyes are deep purple circles in grave contrast with her pale skin. For the first time since I have been here she looks her age. Brooklyn weaves around her legs and the Mother looks down and makes chipmunk noises.

I lean one hip against the counter too, my skirt on backwards, smelling like the sex I just had with her son, and I tell her, "I make a mean shot of tequila. And since it's your tequila you should probably join me."

One ear at a time, the Mother takes off her knotted gold studs, holds them in the palm of her hand.

I tell her to relax. I tell her to freshen up, that I will unload the groceries, to meet me on the back patio when she's ready.

And I tell her to bring her cigarettes. "The good ones," I say.

Freshening up means she will walk by the door that does not close. Marcus asleep, his bare shoulders, his shorts and tee-shirt and shoes on the floor. I have no lie prepared. A *story* is what I usually call it, but a lie is what it is.

She stays leaning against the counter, not quite moving yet, looking at the cat. "That sounds nice," she says.

As soon as she's gone, the first thing I do is take a look inside the cakebox. It is a single-layer sheet cake, white icing, fancy sugar letters, exactly the kind of cake an office of people might pitch in on for someone's going away party, someone's new baby, except where it would ordinarily say *Congratulations* or *Bon Voyage*, it says instead *Happy Birthday Jesus*.

Inside the paper bags are vegetables the colors of bright expensive jewels, the kinds of vegetables most people try and avoid — eggplant, celery, beets, kale, though I don't mind celery, especially with peanut butter stuffed into the open river of the stalk. These are the vegetables she blends with her powders and supplements. These are the vegetables that are keeping her alive.

On the back patio the yellow porch light is right in my face, bright and obscene, illuminating the side of the pink stucco house, the clear gold of the sauza, one clean glass and my dirty one, my bare feet, my inside-out skirt. None of this is what I want to see. I switch off the light, much better.

In pink zip-up bathrobe and delicate white slippers with embroidered flowers, here comes the Mother through the sliding glass door. Even now she doesn't look homey or squashed or quaint. Her hair is down and makeup all removed except for her red lipstick and she sits down in the patio chair next to me and lets out a deep breath that it sounds like she's been holding for a long time. She stares up at the sky, at the stars that shine despite the moon and the light from the houses and the far-off casinos. It's easy to be quiet with the Mother and because we are not talking we can hear things we cannot see, like the tires on asphalt of a car passing by, the whispering tide of endless freeway traffic, a song being played on a nearby piano, rough and choppy, the theme song from *The Wizard of Oz*.

I sing what Dorothy sings. I sing, *We're off to see the Wizard, the Wonderful Wizard of Oz*. I look to see if the Mother is singing too, but she is silent. And as we sit there on our patio chairs before the tequila or cigarettes or talking I can see how really beautiful the Mother is. A dancer at rest. A swan in a lake overrun with mallards. I join her and tilt my head to the sky, the moon up there again, waned considerably from its full bloom.

She does not mention Marcus asleep in the guestroom. I do not mention my skirt. I pour us each a shot and the Mother lights us each a brown-papered Nat Sherman.

One of us says, "To the men."

And the other says, "To the women."

And then the first one of us says, "To us."

And we drink. It is sauza, the good stuff, and we do not need limes or salt. We do not sip it like scotch. We shoot it fast like tough women in the Wild West which, if we were, we'd probably both be prostitutes — the Mother the Madam, and as the Madam she'd probably always smell like perfumed powder and sweat and rosemary oil. When she takes her lips from edge of the glass, there will be a thick smudge of red lipstick remaining there, evidence of her existence, proof that no matter what happens, she is here now.

3.

The dark night is all around. The Mother and I, we are two shots in, two cigarettes deep. She asks if I am okay to drive and I tell her yes, of course, though really I am not sure. Because she doesn't know about the two beers with Marcus earlier. About the passing out. And I have not eaten. But I feel good. I can drive. So even though one of us wears a pink zip-up robe and embroidered white slippers and the other one wears a tee-shirt, sneakers and an inside-out skirt that smells a bit like semen, even so, the two of us, we load into the Dad's quiet Cadillac, with its soft, immaculate dark blue interior to go back to town to pick up the Dad.

I adjust the rearview mirror, my reflection in there. The Mother moves strands of her long red hair, arranging them so they lay at even intervals on her shoulders on the pink fabric of her zip-up robe. The Mother, she is my cargo. And the Dad's Cadillac, this is our vessel. I am the captain.

We are halfway out of the garage, backing into the dark street when the Mother holds up her hands, all ten fingers. "Wait," she says. "Just a moment."

She gets out and glides by in the illumination of the Cadillac's headlights against the wall of the garage. The car chimes a warning, the passenger door ajar. The reminder reminds me that I forgot my purse. I shift back into park and hop out. When I get to the kitchen the Mother says, "Oh, good." She is trying to carry the cake all by herself. Also, the sauza bottle is on the counter and the cap is off.

She says, "I was thinking we should bring the cake."

I am almost positive that I put it back on, that I put the bottle back in the cabinet.

She says, "If Marcus wakes up and sees the cake, he is certain to help himself, don't you think?"

There is a little bit of frosting on the side of her lip.

I say, "I forgot my purse. Hold on."

I sneak up to the guestroom door and push it all the way open, the shush of door against carpet. Brooklyn is curled into Marcus's sleeping heap of a body. I spot my purse right away. On the floor. Which I never do because leaving your purse on the floor is bad luck, my grandma always said. Superstitious, sure, but it makes some kind of sense. When I pick up the purse everything jumbles around in there loud, keys and change and tic-tacs all crashing together in the quiet of the room. Brooklyn jumps off the bed and I say sorry. The heap of Marcus under the bedspread moves. And then the heap of Marcus under the bedspread farts, and I freeze. He's waking up. He farts every morning first thing before he gets out of bed.

Sleepy-voiced he says, "Remind me later to tell you about the turtles."

I wait until his breathing slows back down, then sneak away, the door shushing against carpet. In the Great Room the Mother is letting Brooklyn lick a tiny bit of white frosting off her finger. She does not ask about Marcus. We carry the cake again, me on my side, the Mother on hers, back to the car, back to the trunk, cool and safe and flat.

We are out of the garage, down the driveway, down the street, past the pink houses, through the guardless gate, down the two-lane highway, past the *Liquor!* store and out onto the rushing freeway. Everything red lights and white lights. Everything moving. Far off are the casinos, bright and warm in the cool desert night, like one big campfire leading the way.

The Mother says, "I feel a little tipsy."

She says, "I feel good."

I am busy focusing. I keep my eyes on the road, aim the quiet Cadillac for the perfect place between the white lines at either side.

She says, "I see you squinting." And she's right.

I am squinting at the green highway signs, each one as it heads for us on the side of the road, then moves past and disappears.

"You should probably wear glasses if you have them," she says. "Because I am not quite ready to die."

I keep my eyes on the in-between place of the white lines while the Mother digs in my purse. I remind myself to breathe. Next to me are the moving around sounds of the things that live at the bottom of my purse, keys and change and tic-tacs.

She says, "What am I looking for here?"

She says, "Aha."

The Mother hands me the big round wire frames I never wear, unflattering and ancient, awful just awful, left over from my last year of high school. I know not to look at my reflection in the rearview.

The Mother says, "There."

She says, "That's better."

And fuck if she's not right. The taillights in front of me are now perfectly shaped red rectangles. The buildings in the distance are sharp-edged little boxes of plaster and neon and glass. And the moon, following us still, is cres-cent bright, always there, all the time, even the parts you cannot see. I roll down the window to get it closer, just a bit.

The Mother continues digging in my purse. She says, "There's gum in here. Let's have some gum."

We sit and drive and breathe. We chew gum. The campfire of light getting closer. We are one car in a row of cars moving fast between the lines as we head for the Dad and downtown Las Vegas. We are a river of light in the desert darkness. We are a body in motion. The Mother looks forward out the windshield, her long red hair flying. I keep my hands at two and ten on the wheel.

The Mother starts talking. She says, "In the driver's manual they tell you it's safest to steer at three and nine, but I'm with you. Two and ten feels best to me."

The Mother points north, ahead of us, just past the Vegasy part of Vegas. She is smacking her gum. She says, "See that space in the skyline there past the Strip?"

She says they are building a building there, or are about to.

She says, "Some big-time developer is building it. Some mucky muck." It will have three legs that reach up into the sky, she tells me, and on top of the legs will be a restaurant and amusement park. And it will be tall, very tall, a thousand feet high, the tallest building around by far.

"An amusement park," she says. "Imagine that."

Her hands are folded in her lap, and she does not look at me. But when she talks about the new building I see her fingers unfold and straighten, like her hands are explaining something her words cannot.

I look away from the between-the-lines place and up into the space in the skyline, the empty space I can see perfectly well. The Mother grows the building up out of thin air. And I can see it. Perfectly awkward on its spider thin legs, impossible to ignore, amusement park screams coming from the top, screams that scatter like birds.

She says, "It's going to change everything."

I should be looking at the in-between place but we are both of us staring at the skyline.

"Let's go look at it," I say. "At whatever's there now."

Off the freeway, we drive up Las Vegas Blvd, through the heart of the campfire light, past Caesar's Palace, the Bellagio, all the way up to the chain-link perimeter of the building that isn't there yet.

This part of Vegas is different. I notice right away. We are a ways up from the Strip and the street is older, darker, with beat-up parking meters lining the sidewalk. It smells more like a city too, like sewage and wet garbage and rot. The trash in the street and against the curb is normal trash, fast food wrappers and plastic bags, not porn. I can see a few pawn shops, a video store, an old decrepit market. When we get out of the Dad's Cadillac, I am careful to lock the doors. I cannot see the mountains but I know they are there.

The Mother and I, we stand together at the base of the thing, concrete and steel, the fenced-off beginnings of three legs that will reach up to the sky. I take my chewed up gum wad and stick it on the fence. The Mother sees me, does it too.

She says, "Maybe when it's time I can take the elevator all the way to the top and then jump off."

I look up to the invisible top and picture the Mother in her pink zip-up robe sailing through the sky, diving like a bird from an outstretched branch. Without meaning to, I picture Brooklyn jumping too. And the Dad. The three of them together, falling to the Earth.

Beside me the Mother is looking up, her neck craned, hair loose and long down her back, eyes aimed high up into the dark. The little bit of frosting gone.

I say, "It's going to be hideous."

And the Mother says, "Yes. Probably it will. But think of the view."

She draws her hand across the imaginary skyscape, and paints me a picture. "Close your eyes. Are they closed? Okay. So the mountains would be to the north."

In my mind, the outline of the mountains dip and peak and join again, like dark clouds rolling in from offshore.

Like she can see what I'm seeing, she says, "Good."

"And over there," says the Mother. "That would be the Strip. There's Caesar's Palace."

In my mind, I see the Dad, exchanging money for chips, chips for money, working hard behind some metal bars in his black vest.

"He's going to love the cake," she says. "I know he will."

I am starting to get cold, goosebumps on my legs, so I

peek. I can't help it. The Mother has eyelids where her eyes should be.

She says, "And over there, far off, past all the lights, where it is dark. That is just desert. Just desert and sand and the animals that live in it."

She says, "Even though it's different, the desert here reminds me of where I grew up. Medicine Bowl, Wyoming."

In my mind, I try to picture what a place called Medicine Bowl would look like.

She says, "In Medicine Bowl there were more cows than people. So many cows that whenever you went anywhere you'd end up waiting while a river of cattle crossed the road. My dad said it drove him crazy but I think he loved it. Just sitting there in the car waiting for the cows to herd past."

The Mother comes down off the top of the building and opens her eyes.

A car comes down the street, headlights on us, then off illuminating the Mother's naked ankles and embroidered slippers.

She says, "I should have brought a sweater."

A man walks out of the dilapidated market. I can see him perfectly well. He walks up the sidewalk, talking to himself, his shoulder-length gray hair messy under a knit cap, beat-up white sneakers on his feet. In his hand is a black plastic bag heavy with something that sounds like two bottles clanging. To one of us or the other of us, he whistles. He says, "Yes." His head turns on his body so he can get a good look, so he can keep looking as he passes.

Instinctively we cross the dark street and head for the light of the dilapidated market. Through a turnstile, past the man at the register in a Santa's hat, past the glowing Christmas lights of a Kahlua display, walking on the checkerboard linoleum, stained and chipped and sticky. A radio somewhere plays an instrumental version of *Jingle Bell Rock*. With my inside-out skirt and the Mother's robe and slippers we probably look like we belong.

Even here, at a filthy market in the bad part of Vegas, there are slot machines. Three of them, aging, dirty, scratched up, they're covered in tinsel and red and green lights.

The Mother says, "Well, we should probably play one. Just to see."

I shake my purse around, listening for the change down there at the bottom.

"We're just killing time," she says.

"Yes," I say, holding out a quarter. "Killing time."

The Mother says, "You first."

I take a deep breath. The Santa man at the register watches us. I pick the machine farthest from the turnstile, feed it my quarter and pull the handle. I hold in my breath. We watch the pictures wheel by. I exhale. Nothing. I dig again to the bottom of my purse and retrieve another quarter.

"Now me," the Mother says.

She pulls the lever. I hold my breath. We stare together into the face of the machine. We wait to see what will happen. The pictures wheel by. They settle. I exhale. And nothing.

I shake my purse again, but the man at the register with the Santa hat says, "Here. Allow me."

He digs in his pocket and hands me a quarter. His hands are small and calloused, nails bitten down to the quick.

He says, "You know. Merry Christmas. Whatever."

The Mother is bouncing in her slippers on the checkerboard linoleum. She says, "You again. You go."

I stand in front of the last slot machine.

The Santa man says, "Yeah. Go get 'em."

So I pull the handle and the wheels are spinning and I know I am forgetting to breathe. The wheels are spinning and my palms are sweating and I wipe them on my skirt and when I do, I know. I know I am going to win. And the Mother knows it too.

And as the cherries and lemons and 7-ups go rushing by the Mother says, "I do this every time. I always hope."

WELCOME TO SAMSARA

We were not *beach people*. Neither of us had what's known as a *swimsuit body*. Plus, Bert didn't particularly like sand, and I hated the way my feet looked in flip-flops, really anyone's feet. Flip-flops are not the best venue for viewing feet in general. But I'd been ten weeks pregnant, and then we lost the baby, and, after, I wasn't doing so good. Pretty much, I just wanted to die.

Bert didn't know what to do with me.

Every day for two weeks, he asked how he could make me happy. I couldn't possibly answer him. He tried chocolate and flowers and finally a little zirconia heart on a gold chain, I guess because those were the ways men made women happy on television. I couldn't say what I really wanted was for Bert to have some decent semen meet up with a healthy egg and to please bring the zygote to me in a petri dish: that would make me happy. But I didn't want to hurt his feelings, so I accepted the sweet, ordinary gifts he gave me, and when he was sleeping or watching basketball, I'd toss them out in the big gray garbage bin on the side of our house.

It's true I wanted to die, but I didn't want to do the dirty work, so I hung around in my body to breathe and cry and hate the world.

Bert suggested meditation.

Far as I could tell, meditation was about sitting and not doing anything and I was already doing that most days, so why the hell not. It's about breathing, he told me. Just breathe until you think of nothing. So I sat on the bed and breathed. I kept thinking of stuff. The next day, I tried again. I sat and breathed, and it was better. I think I almost did it. I was almost nothing! And then the phone rang down the hall and I screamed, *You suck!* and I was something again.

Next day, Bert suggested a counselor.

"You think I fucking need a therapist?"

I was in my pajamas sitting on the edge of our messy unmade bed. Out the window, three big crows were perched on the bent top boughs of a pine tree across the street, their black claws clutched firm on the swaying branches. It seemed like a good life to be a crow, the bullies of the bird world.

"No, not a therapist," Bert said. He was standing in the doorway. "A counselor. For stuff like this they're called counselors. They counsel you. They don't therapute you, or therapize, I'm not sure what the right word there would be..."

The biggest of the three crows swiveled and cocked his bird head, one black eye, I swear, looking right at me.

"Did you see that?" I said. "I think he saw me."

"More like a guidance counselor. But for grown up people, you know, going through the stuff that we did. What happened here. With us." Bert sat down next to me on the bed and tried to see what I was seeing out the window.

I smelled it right away. The sour, charred, dead smell that piggybacks on clothes and skin.

"Are you smoking again?" I ask.

"No," he says. "Just a little. Barely at all."

She was an older woman. I forget her name. We only

went once. I remember she wore a yellow knit cardigan; her eyes were a rheumy blue. Everything about her said death. She showed us to her office, a room without windows or plants, sat Bert and me down in matching uncomfortable blue office chairs and listened to our story. Bad eggs, tiny testicles, blah, blah, blah, then, pills, injections, artificial insemination, then, at last, morning sickness, sore breasts, blah, blah, blah, that good part lasting just long enough to trust it, and then, blam, it was gone.

The counselor listened, leaning forward in her chair, sipping something from a ceramic mug. When I was done, she spoke with an infuriating calm, her voice so close to a whisper I had to lean forward too.

"Cheryl," she said. The sound of my name in her mouth made me want to eat her face off. "What a journey you've been on, both of you." She looked at Bert. She looked back at me. All of us now leaning forward in our chairs, like logs on a pyre. "These kinds of events can be hard."

Bert reached over and held my hand. It was awkward because we both had these wooden office chair armrests between us, but still, I knew him well enough to know when he reached over he wasn't saying, *Yes, this is hard.* He was saying, *Yes, you're right, honey, she's an idiot, just keep it together a little bit longer.*

She said some other stuff.

She said, "Sometimes it helps to honor the event in some way." What event? It wasn't a President's Day Sale. "Many of my other families found it helpful to buy a little figurine, something to keep around the house, to honor the event. Something to remember." She pointed to a white ceramic angel sitting on the top of a messy book-shelf, its wings spread wide, head bowed in reverence, tiny angel hands palm to palm in prayer.

Didn't she know? Remembering wasn't really the problem; it was the forgetting I was having trouble with.

"Cheryl, do you think it might be helpful for you to have a keepsake like this? It's okay to tell us. This is a safe place."

Perhaps she could feel the hate lasers shooting out of my eyeballs. Perhaps not. Either way, it was time to go.

"Yes," I said. "What a good idea." I stood up. "We'll go get that now. Thank you."

Bert stood up too. "Great," he said. "I think we're all set here." He was still holding my hand. I couldn't let go quite yet.

The counselor rose to her feet with us. She said, "We have some more time if you'd like to keep talking."

"Wonderful," he said again. "This was great." Bert and I, we've always been good counterbalancing each other at our worst. "Thank you so much," he said. "Thanks." He reached out to shake her hand with his free hand and for a moment the three of us formed a human chain, like together we might break out into song to oppose senseless killings or an oppressive regime; but what had happened to us wasn't anything like that: it was only a miscarriage, the single quiet slipping away of something that wasn't quite something enough yet.

The counselor broke away first, dropping Bert's hand and smoothing her skirt, or perhaps she just wiped his hand sweat off her palm.

As I grabbed my raincoat and purse from the side of the chair, she said one last thing.

"One last thing," she said. "For families, couples, in your situation, sometimes it helps to take a breath from your life. Yes? A little vacation, just the two of you. Enjoy yourselves. Eat a nice chicken dinner. Drink some wine." She said more stuff as we walked out, who knows what. I knew to stop listening at her best piece of advice.

Bert belly flops into the Royal Papaya Resort's chemical blue pool water, brimming with chlorine and probably, let's face it, at least one person's urine. The cool water splashes onto my bare legs, stretched out on a Royal Papaya lounge chair. A pale thin boy with goggles and a kickboard struggles to stay afloat in the wake of Bert's capsizing body. I don't feel too bad for the kid. It's the same unsupervised boy from check-in yesterday who kept clipping and unclipping the red ropes from the stanchions until the whole thing fell over on its side and sent a loud clang throughout the tropical open-air lobby.

Bert heaves his body onto the pool's rim and clambers up onto his feet, then performs some kind of running side leap back into the pool. The water is tossed up against the pool's concrete lip and sloshes back and forth, splashing my legs again. An older couple across the pool lies on their side-by-side lounge chairs reading a newspaper. On their heads are matching crisp white ball caps with the hotel logo, a fat gold papaya wearing a crown. They give me a look like Bert is my responsibility and he's out of control and could I please do something to ensure he no longer invades their equatorial peace with splashed water spots on their precious morning reading material. I smile and wave and think, *Fuck you so much.*

Bert doggie-paddles to the metal railing on my side of the pool, which in the pictures on the Royal Papaya web-site appears enormous, as big as a lake, but in person is as big as a regular pool.

He limps towards the empty lounger next to me. "I think I stubbed my toe when I did that cartwheel."

"Is that what that was?" I say.

The pool waiter walks by in sunglasses, surf shorts and a tank top. It's hard to tell he's a waiter; he looks more like a lifeguard, except he's carrying a round tray. I order an iced coffee with Kahlua because it's morning but also it's Hawaii.

"You know a cartwheel is on your hands, right?" I say.

"No, I don't think so. That's not right." Bert towels off his chest and hair. "Why is it called a cartwheel if you need your hands. Carts don't have hands."

I have no reply.

Next to me, a few lounge chairs over, is a woman my age wearing a great big straw hat and a very small string bikini. She's drinking from a champagne flute and she is on her cell phone. She has not stopped talking since she sat down next to me and I now know her entire life story. I know, for instance, that she is married to a man named Hugh. I know that Hugh has finally switched dentists. I know they took this vacation alone expressly to have sex because, since the birth of their only child, they have managed to fornicate on a total of four occasions.

Bert's reclined on the lounger, wrapped up in a towel and his eyes are closed. He has a white glop of sunscreen un-rubbed in on his forehead and the tip of his nose. He must feel me looking at him. "This is incredible," he says. "Why haven't we been doing this all along? We should come back next year, and the year after that… every year. Let's never stop coming back here."

When a couple goes to Hawaii, I'm pretty sure they're supposed to have sex. Not me though, I couldn't do it. It'd been two months since our President's Day Sale, but my body still felt distended and foreign, my clothes fit wrong, like they were someone else's clothes. Sex only served to remind my body that it was a different body than it used to be. My old body liked sex; this new body preferred to be the basecamp for a brain. Physicality was not to be trusted: without warning, it could fail.

Instead of having the sex we should have been having, Bert would doze in front of our room's giant flat screen TV and I would lace up my sneakers and wander the maze of the outdoor market near our hotel, a great big Tiki-themed tourist extravaganza. I zigzagged through the stands, and thought about purchasing rainbow magnets and waterfall mugs and macadamia nut sampler packs, gifts for friends and family that I knew myself well enough to know I'd never actually give away: the souvenirs would sit in their original bags on a shelf in the hall closet for years until I moved or died or threw them out. I didn't ever want to buy anything, but I went back each afternoon to disappear. I love to disappear in a crowd. I love it the way other people love attention. Also, there was an enormous ancient banyan tree in the middle of the market, a big beautiful mess of cascading branches and roots and trunks that kept the place shaded and cool. Underneath that tree, each afternoon, I would sit for a little while and hope for my life to make sense again. Then when it didn't, I'd head back to the hotel.

That night, waiting for a table in the dining room, we trip into a conversation with another tourist about swimming in the ocean. His name is Walt and he's in his sixties, and his wife Darlene looks a good bit younger.

"It's really quite a treat," he says.

His arms are deeply tanned and hairy and he's wearing a short-sleeved brown and green tiki-patterned aloha shirt that shows them off and his wife has a matching off-the-shoulder muumuu.

"We haven't been in the water yet," I say. I check my watch. It's been twenty minutes already. I try to make eye contact with the hostess, but she's some kind of expert at gaze avoidance.

"In the pool, we have," Bert says. "We've played in the water at the pool. Remember? We swam around."

"Right, honey," I say. "But I think this man…"

"Walt," he says.

"Walt, he's talking about the ocean."

"Oh indeed," Walt says. "Screw the pool. You folks could be in a pool anywhere, but you can only be in the water in Hawaii, *in Hawaii.*"

"Well, I'm not that into sand," Bert says. "Each piece is so tiny. It always gets everywhere."

Times like this I wish I carried a compact in my purse so I could stare into it and pat my cheeks with powder.

"You know what I'm saying," Bert says. "Chafing and whatnot. When I was a kid I'd get this rash inside my shorts…"

What on earth could be taking so long? Maybe they're out back building the table with fresh felled palm wood as we speak.

"Yes, sir," Walt says. "Something about being in the water here just takes the starch right out of you."

Behind the hostess station is an enormous aquarium filled with bright fish and their calming lackadaisical fins. Walt's words take a swim through the tank before they make it to my ears. "Sorry. What do you mean?" I say.

"You know," Walt says. "Whatever's bothering you or whatever you're worried about, it all just disappears," he says.

"Yes," Darlene says. "Isn't that true?" She is gripping her husband's arm in acknowledgment of their shared

142

understanding. "I feel the same way after I come back from the mall. I don't know what it is. I feel so relaxed."

Right after the miscarriage, whenever I had to leave the house for groceries or gin or toilet paper, I kept a straight line of an almost-smile on my lips so everyone would think I was *Doing Okay*, which was exactly what everyone who knew what happened would ask. Picture how their faces would squish up into puckered bunches when the question left their lips. Here, in Hawaii, nobody knew me. I could be anyone here for any reason. I could be here to celebrate something happy, not to get away from something sad. It begged the question of the people around me. I watched them walk on packed sidewalks with melting ice cream cones in their hands. I watched them rub shiny oil on their jiggly bellies and thighs, then untie their bikini halter strings to avoid unsightly tan lines. I watched them play tennis, the bright green ball smacked back and forth in the hot sun. I couldn't tell a damn thing. All of us were here in this beautiful place for our own reasons, and we'd never know who came here to remember and who came here to forget.

This morning when I wake up there's a lot of hubbub down a ways on the beach. A man, a tourist from Idaho or maybe South Dakota — *Oh shoot*, a woman told me, *I can't remember* — he went for an early swim and never came back. *Snorkeler found him bumping up against the rocks over there*, someone else said. Parked on the white sand were a couple police cars and a big white medical examiner van. A handful of hotel guests like me scattered along the cement path poolside as the sun crept its way higher in the empty blue sky. I thought of Walt and his aloha shirt and how hairy and tan his arms were, and I hoped it wasn't him.

After, I head for the breakfast buffet because I'm supposed to meet Bert there, but I'm not that hungry. Even coffee doesn't sound good. I walk past the smells of kept-warm bacon and burning toast in a toaster and eggs becoming an omelette in a pan. Bert waves from his table when he sees me. Before I can even sit down in my chair, I smell it: he's been smoking again. I don't say anything.

"What?" he says. "I had one. We're on vacation!"

"Death doesn't need your help," I say. "Cut it out."

I steal a piece of melon from his plate.

"You hear about that guy?" Bert says. "The ocean swimmer? Man, those waves will just eat you alive."

I steal a piece of pineapple this time.

"Like I said," he says. "I'm all about the pool. Perfectly happy with the pool."

An arm materializes in front of me, uprights my down-turned water glass and fills it all the way up. The arm disappears.

"I bet the last thing that guy thought was, *Crap. I should've swum in the pool.*"

"That's not funny," I say. "That guy could have been someone's husband, or somebody's dad."

"I'm not being funny," Bert says. He offers me the last piece of fruit, a sad-looking shriveled green grape. I shake my head.

"I bet he thought that," he says. "That's what I'd be thinking."

Wandering the market in my sneakers this afternoon, I find a souvenir ceramic tile for sale. It has a pair of flip-flops painted on it and above that in blue letters it says, *Aloha Style – Leave your shoes at the door.* Yes, I think. Yes! It's time for a change. I've never been a shoes-off kind of person, but maybe I could be. Nice and tidy. No shoe muck in the house. No more muck! Without all that shoe muck to clean up, I'd have so much more free time. Imagine the possibilities. I could learn to paint or sing or maybe teach myself karate. I could be whoever I wanted to be. I don't have to be the person I was before, the person I am right now.

"How much for this tile?" I say.

A large Hawaiian woman sits on a stool next to the cart, reading a folded up magazine. She does not look up to see what I am asking about. "Twenty dollars."

"It's a tile," I say.

"Yup. Twenty dollars."

"Am I supposed to bargain with you? That's how this works right? I say, how about twelve, and you say, eighteen, and I say fifteen, and you say sold?"

She keeps reading, kicks one flip flop off and scratches her left foot with her right big toe. Slips the flip-flop back on.

"Twenty dollars," she says.

Two girls in bikini tops and short shorts wander up to the cart and start trying on pooka shell bracelets.

"Fifteen?" I say.

"Twenty dollars," she says. She turns a glossy magazine page.

I suck at this.

The bikini top girls whisper to each other, they hold their arms up in the air and watch the white shell bracelets slide down their dark tan skin. One of them, the brunette, has a stomach that is tan and taut, a butt almost succulent in its perfection, and I momentarily understand why some men are such fuck-crazy assholes. My only consolation is knowing one day she'll hit forty.

"Eighteen," I say.

"Twenty dollars," the merchant says.

Oh fuck me. "Fine. Twenty dollars."

Flip-flop tile in my purse, I walk back to the hotel, through the open-air lobby, and on my way to our room I change my mind and head, at last, for the ocean instead. I follow the cement path that hugs the Royal Papaya property.

The path spits me out onto a skinny crescent of sand smack up against the water where the beachfront is alive with chaos. Bright rectangles of beach towels, striped umbrellas planted in the sand leaning like flowers toward the sun, beach chairs, boogie boards, buckets and shovels, snorkel masks and foot fins, coolers and blankets and canvas bags brimming with sunscreen and bottled water and thick books to read, and the whole damn place is overrun with kids — a fat baby sits eating handfuls of sand, a toddler on a dad's broad shoulders galloping to the edge of the water, a pregnant woman, her belly erupting between her bikini top and bottom, sits at the shoreline building a sandcastle with a little boy.

Month after month, then year after year, the women around me bloomed with pregnancy, then motherhood, then they'd ask me to come over for coffee and listen to their complaints about breastfeeding and not sleeping and here, will you hold the baby while I pee. There were times when I felt like it might actually kill me to fake one more smile for another friend's *I'm pregnant* news. But I kept at it because I hoped that if I tried hard to be a good friend, a good wife, a good person I could circumvent biology and be granted a baby in my womb. I wholly believed with the right combination of patience and forced decency I would become one of the people with tired eyes and a car floor messy with crushed up cheesy goldfish and a refrigerator cluttered with unintelligible smeary art.

Waves blast the sand and the wind pushes fat white clouds across the island and the people around me shout and laugh and sit and read and walk back and forth from the water, and I understand that hope is a lie. It's a lie we tell ourselves to avoid the pain of what is; and sometimes, like with me, what is is what is not.

Right then, it comes for me: a heave of bottomless grief rises up from somewhere achingly deep, from the core of the earth, and with every fiber of my being I comprehend with an impossible certainty that Bert and I will not ever be able to have children: it is not going to happen. The truth of this knowing makes my lungs stop working; it hits me in the throat and then the back of the knees like a baseball bat and I don't have any sense of where my body is in space. The truth of it is so all consuming, I am gone. It sinks me.

My body walks itself to the stretch of beach where they found the disappeared swimmer. It's an absolutely gorgeous spot — palm trees bending to blue water against white sand, black rocks piled up along the shore. I think of the man who died and what Bert said and, I don't know, maybe he has it all wrong. Maybe the last thing the swimmer thought was, *If I have to go, no better place than this.*

· · ·

The first cool bite of salt water licks at my feet. I tell myself that's as far as I'll go because I don't have a towel with me and I'm not wearing a swimsuit and someone dressed in sneakers, shorts and a tank top can't just walk into the sea, but the water comes for me anyway — it climbs to my ankles, then crawls up my calves, inching up over my knees, lapping at my thighs until it overtakes my hips, encircles my waist, rises to embrace my breasts and shoulders, and then the ocean cradles my head as I lay back and let it float me. The white clouds drift, fluffed up in the blue sky, cool water around the crown of my head, the hypnotic sound of wave after wave slapping the shore, the hiss of crashed water crawling up the sand and slipping back down, wind breathing through the long fronds of palms, and for what might be a second or an hour or a year I disappear from myself. I do not think about my clothes being wet; I do not think about what I lost or what I will never have. The water feels warm now and it bobs me up and down on its surface. Listen, it says. You are here for this instant floating in an ocean wrapping a planet wildly spinning and in revolution around a fire hot sun of a star. You are a body breathing in, a body breathing out. You are breathing. You are breath. You are, at last, nothing.

Acknowledgments

These stories were written and re-written over the course of twelve years. I can't possibly thank all the folks who were involved in their creation and re-shaping without keeping you up all night long. Writers, teachers, friends, family, strangers overheard on the street. ... I owe you my greatest thanks.

My deep gratitude to M. Allen Cunningham and Atelier26 for making this book possible, for making the stories better, and for making the dream a reality. Mark, you are one hell of an editor and a publisher.

Thank you to Literary Arts, the Regional Arts & Culture Council and the Oregon Arts Commission for financial support during the writing of these stories. Thank you to Soapstone, and the Sitka Center for Art & Ecology for providing me the time and space to write in two of my most favorite places on earth. And thank you to Flip Brophy for always taking the time.

Thank you to the wise and generous teachers I've had the great fortune to work with over the years, especially Les Plesko, the first to show unbridled enthusiasm for my work; Lisa Glatt, who gave me the courage to write about anything and the permission to take my writer self seriously; and finally to Tom Spanbauer, who provided the space for me to attempt on the page what he is a master at — baring the darkest recesses of a heart with generosity and fearlessness.

Thank you to all the Dangerous Writers who were at the table when several of the stories were written or edited, who encouraged me every Thursday night to dive down to the messiest, most beautiful places in me and bring back my best sentences, (especially Colin, Kevin, Gigi, Brad, Holly, Charles and Adam, with a shout out to Jacob Morehead who said casually, "What about the balloons?"); <u>all</u> you DWs — you are my second family. With an extra special thank you to Kathleen Lane, whose smart, thoughtful feedback has made me an infinitely better writer, and whose friendship has made me a better human.

Thank you to Andrea Crimmins for infinite emotional support before, during, and after the writing of these stories.

Thank you to Brian Lindstrom & Cheryl Strayed for demonstrating years ago what it really means to live the dream, and for their beautiful humanness, support and friendship.

Thank you to Barbara Turner, one of the best writers I've ever known and the person who taught me to say, *Fuck what you think I should do. I'm doing it this way.*

Thank you to Cynthia Barrett, the most encouraging, supportive boss imaginable, who never hesitated to give me time off for a residency or writing class or teaching opportunity: you are directly responsible for this book being in the world.

Thank you to Jordan Foster, who never stopped trying to find a way to help.

Thank you to Victoria Ensz, for extraordinary care of my son while finishing the first draft of this book.

Thank you to Jimyo Culnan, my secret-weapon guru.

Thank you to my mom and my dad for their praise and support and for never saying, *What's taking you so long?* And thank you to Bill and Marge Padian for hours of babysitting so I could write and edit.

Thank you to all my friends: I am blessed with a truckload of you. I'm a far better person for knowing you. True.

My biggest thanks are reserved for Brian Padian, who somehow incredibly is the person I get to spend my life with, who encourages me and kicks my ass and loves me unconditionally no matter my imperfections; and to Nicholas and Frieda, who make everything better everyday.

CPSIA information can be obtained at www.ICGtesting.com
Printed in the USA
LVOW07s2128101115

461986LV00003B/190/P

9 780989 3023